A Cherokee Knight.
A Dragon Slayer.

Sarah couldn't keep her eyes off Adam. He stood before her, his thumbs hooked in his pockets—a stance that made the female in her take notice.

He took a step toward her. "We still haven't talked about what happened earlier."

"We're just friends." The statement sounded foolish, even to her own ears.

"I keep telling myself that. We're just friends. There's nothing happening between us." He laughed, a rough-textured sound that faded as quickly as it came on. "That's a lie, at least for me. I can't help myself. I want you. And I can't pretend that I don't." He moved closer, until they were only inches apart. "You're my midnight seduction, sweet Sarah."

Her heart thumped wildly. She wanted to kiss him, seduce him, feel him branding her skin. Mist and moonlight, she thought. Fairy tales and fantasies. She craved all of that and more.

But wanting Adam didn't mean she had the courage to take him.

Dear Reader,

Welcome to the world of Silhouette Desire, where you can indulge yourself every month with romances that can only be described as passionate, powerful and provocative!

The ever-fabulous Ann Major offers a *Cowboy Fantasy*, July's MAN OF THE MONTH. Will a fateful reunion between a Texas cowboy and his ex-flame rekindle their fiery passion? In *Cherokee*, Sheri WhiteFeather writes a compelling story about a Native American hero who, while searching for his Cherokee heritage, falls in love with a heroine who has turned away from hers.

The popular miniseries BACHELOR BATTALION by Maureen Child marches on with *His Baby!*—a marine hero returns from an assignment to discover he's a father. The tantalizing Desire miniseries FORTUNES OF TEXAS: THE LOST HEIRS continues with *The Pregnant Heiress* by Eileen Wilks, whose pregnant heroine falls in love with the investigator protecting her from a stalker.

Alexandra Sellers has written an enchanting trilogy, SONS OF THE DESERT: THE SULTANS, launching this month with *The Sultan's Heir*. A prince must watch over the secret child heir to the kingdom along with the child's beautiful mother. And don't miss Bronwyn Jameson's Desire debut—an intriguing tale involving a self-made man who's *In Bed with the Boss's Daughter*.

Treat yourself to all six of these heart-melting tales of Desire—and see inside for details on how to enter our Silhouette Makes You a Star contest.

Enjoy!

Joan Marlow Golan

Joan Marlow Golan
Senior Editor, Silhouette Desire

Please address questions and book requests to:
Silhouette Reader Service
U.S.: 3010 Walden Ave., P.O. Box 1325, Buffalo, NY 14269
Canadian: P.O. Box 609, Fort Erie, Ont. L2A 5X3

Cherokee
SHERI WHITEFEATHER

Published by Silhouette Books
America's Publisher of Contemporary Romance

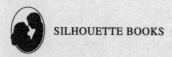 SILHOUETTE BOOKS

ISBN 0-373-76376-X

CHEROKEE

Copyright © 2001 by Sheree Henry-WhiteFeather

Books by Sheri WhiteFeather

Silhouette Desire

Warrior's Baby #1248
Skyler Hawk: Lone Brave #1272
Jesse Hawk: Brave Father #1278
Cheyenne Dad #1300
Night Wind's Woman #1332
Tycoon Warrior #1364
Cherokee #1376

SHERI WHITEFEATHER

lives in Southern California and enjoys ethnic dining, summer powwows and visiting art galleries and vintage clothing stores near the beach. Since her one true passion is writing, she is thrilled to be a part of the Silhouette Desire line. When she isn't writing, she often reads until the wee hours of the morning.

Sheri also works as a leather artisan with her Muscogee Creek husband. They have one son and a menagerie of pets, including a pampered English bulldog and four equally spoiled Bengal cats. She would love to hear from her readers. You may write to her at: P.O. Box 5130, Orange, California 92863-5130.

To the Cherokees who inspired this story—
Annie Dear-Johnson for her strength and sensitivity;
Lisa Kelly and her daughter Mandi for their beauty and
heart; Kona Bruckner and her children, Amy, Bryon
and Jeremiah for their triumph; Christine Tevis and her
sons, Bobby, Bruce and Bryon (my favorite little artist)
for following Windrunner's path.

I would also like to acknowledge Barbara Carlton
for teaching her son about his Cherokee heritage and
Barbara Ann Tucker, my Texas friend, for the lovely letters
and powwow pictures. And to another Barbara, my
proud and supportive mother-in-law, many thanks for
encouraging us to consider alternative medicine whenever
one of us is ailing. Unfortunately we don't always listen,
but the characters in this book took your advice to heart.

And finally to the countless readers out there
expressing an interest in the American Indian culture,
this recipe is for you:

INDIAN FRY BREAD
(from various sources)

Cornmeal or flour for dusting board
2 cups flour
1/2 tsp salt
1/2 tsp baking powder
1/2 cup instant dry milk
3/4 cup water
Oil or shortening for deep frying

Dust pastry board. In a mixing bowl, stir flour, baking
powder, salt and powdered milk. Add water in small
amounts, stirring until the mixture reaches the consistency
of bread dough. Knead until smooth and elastic. Cover and
let rest for ten minutes. Heat oil or shortening in a deep
frying pan. Pull off a palm-size mound of dough, roll into
a ball, then flatten into a 6-inch disc. Fry one at a time
on both sides until golden. Serve hot, sprinkled with
powdered sugar, drizzled with honey or covered
with taco fixings. Makes about 4 servings.

One

Sarah Cloud entered the break room, her productive day nearing its end. She didn't own Ventura West, a successful skin care salon in the San Fernando Valley, but she took pride in working there. She enjoyed soothing her clients with a refreshing mask and a quiet shoulder massage. They relied on her to make them feel whole, to sweep them away from the hustle and bustle of their harried L.A. lives, if only for an hour each week.

Removing a small container of orange juice from the refrigerator, she looked up. Tina Carpenter, the sweet but air-brained receptionist, stood in the doorway.

"You're never going to believe who's here," the young woman said, her eyes wide and bright. "It's that doctor-type guy from the clinic next door."

Sarah smiled, amused by Tina's definition of the holistic practitioner. Of course it wasn't his profession that mattered to the women in the salon. All were in agreement that their new neighbor was by far one of the most attractive men they had ever seen. Sarah had no idea what to think, since she had yet to catch even a quick glimpse of him. Not that she cared. Southern California overflowed with tall, tan, muscular men.

Tina flashed an excited grin. "Guess what? He wants to talk to you. And he even said it's personal. I wonder if he's going to ask you on a date or something."

Baffled, Sarah capped her orange juice. A date? With a woman he'd never even met? Not likely. "Are you sure it's me he wants to talk to?" This wouldn't be the first time Tina had misconstrued a message. The receptionist was the owner's niece—an inept but permanent employee.

"Of course I'm sure, silly." Tina grabbed her arm. "Come on. He's waiting."

Sarah approached the reception area, then slowed her pace when she saw him. He stood near the front window, almost out of place amid the elegant ambiance of the salon. He wasn't what she had expected. He wore dark indigo jeans and a blue button-down shirt, the sleeves rolled to his elbows. But it wasn't his ranch-style attire that made her stop and stare. She knew immediately that the color of his skin hadn't been enhanced by the sun, his golden complexion and strong, chiseled profile suddenly reminding her of home. An uncomfortable reminder.

When he turned, their eyes met. And then held. She wanted to look away, but couldn't. He was too unusual to be considered classically handsome. Each riveting feature battled for dominance—eyes too deep, a mouth too full, cheekbones so prominent they could have been sculpted from clay.

He was a mixed blood, she realized. But how mixed she couldn't quite tell. He wore his hair long, but it was brown instead of black, secured at his nape in a thick ponytail.

Sarah took a deep breath, more uncomfortable than ever. She hated being reminded of home.

He came toward her, his height overwhelming. She had been wrong. California wasn't overflowing with men like him. His masculine presence commanded attention, but his smile generated warmth. No wonder no woman within breathing distance could keep her eyes off him. Tina leaned over the reception desk, and Claire, the flamboyant makeup artist, craned her neck to get a good look at his backside.

"Hi," he said. "I'm Adam Paige. I work next door."

Sarah extended her hand, sensing he waited for her to do so. Apparently he had been taught the same protocol. A man didn't touch a woman without invitation, not even in a greeting.

The handshake sent an electrical charge straight up her arm. She drew back quickly, keeping her voice polite and professional. "I'm Sarah Cloud. How can I help you?"

He pushed at his shirtsleeve, shoving it further up his arm. "Vicki Lester suggested I stop by. She's a patient of mine."

Sarah nodded. Vicki was a client of hers, too. And a friend. Vicki lived in the same sprawling apartment complex. "She didn't tell me to expect you," Sarah said, hoping she didn't sound too distrustful. How could her friend neglect to mention this man and all his rugged beauty?

"I saw Vicki this morning," he explained. "After her appointment, we got into a serious conversation. When I told her about what's going on in my life, she thought I should talk to you."

His life? I'm an esthetician, Sarah thought, not a psychologist. If he had problems, the best she could do was ease him with a facial—lift the tension from his forehead, massage the stress from his shoulders.

She glanced up at those broad shoulders and swallowed. Then again, talking might be better. She actually found herself attracted to Adam Paige—a man whose golden complexion and Indian cheekbones reminded her of why she'd left home. "Would you like to sit down?"

He glanced around, caught Tina's eye and returned her smile, indicating to Sarah that the bouncy blond receptionist appeared to be eavesdropping.

"Maybe we could go across the street to the juice bar instead," he said.

"Sure, that's fine." Sarah had some time to spare, and a cold drink sounded good. She'd left her orange juice on the table, and now her mouth felt unusually dry.

He opened the door for her, and they stepped onto the sidewalk in front of the salon. Ventura Boulevard buzzed around them. Late-day traffic gathered at a red light while summer tourists explored what locals simply called the Valley.

Sarah looked over at Adam as they crossed the street, and he sent her a devastating smile. If she hadn't been wearing sensible shoes, she would have tripped over her own feet.

Curious, she glanced down at Adam's feet, wondering what sort of shoes he wore. Lace-up ropers, she saw, California style. No dust, no scuffed toes. In spite of his Western appeal, Adam Paige with the chiseled profile and heart-stopping smile had most likely been born and raised in the Valley.

Sarah lifted her gaze, realizing a case of nerves had set in. Suddenly she felt like the troubled Oklahoma girl she had been. The one who had come to L.A. with nothing more than a battered suitcase and a need to break free of her past.

After Sarah's mother died, her father had found solace in the bottle, drinking his way into oblivion. And as much as she loved her dad, walking away from him had become her only option. She had learned firsthand how deceptive alcoholics could be, how irresponsible and hurtful.

She glanced toward the sky and recalled his last broken promise, the last devastating lie. She'd graduated from high school two weeks before, and had come home from a new full-time job to find her dad in the backyard. He was dressed in grubby clothes, the old jeans and T-shirt he wore when tending the rose bushes that bloomed every summer. The flowers Sarah loved, the only beauty left in their run-down yard.

Standing in the setting sun, she watched her father reach into a planter and dig below the dirt. And then her breath caught, the threat of tears stinging her eyes.

The bottle that glinted in his hand could have been a knife. When he dusted it off, twisted the cap and took a drink, a sharp pain sliced through her—the sickening stab of betrayal.

He turned and their eyes met. And at that painful moment, she knew. He wasn't her father anymore, the man she had once admired, the Cherokee warrior who used to tuck her in at night. Too many scenes like this one had destroyed those warm, tender feelings. For Sarah, there was nothing left but emptiness.

Neither said a word. She didn't accuse, and he didn't apologize. They only stood, staring at each other. His graduation gift to her had been an impassioned promise, an ardent vow of sobriety, and that gift had just been shattered, along with Sarah's eighteen-year-old heart.

"We're here."

Blinking, she turned to see Adam, not her father, watching her. "I'm sorry. What?"

"The juice bar."

"Oh, of course."

Once inside, they ordered their drinks and sat across from each other in a small booth. Sarah fidgeted with her cup. Adam studied her, his gaze scanning the length of her hair.

"Vicki told me that you're originally from Tahlequah," he said. "And that you're registered with the Cherokee Nation."

She stiffened at the mention of her hometown and her heritage, her memories still too close to the edge. "Yes, I am. Is this what you wanted to talk to me about?"

He nodded, his voice tinged with emotion. "I just found out that I was born in Tahlequah and that I'm part Cherokee, too. I know that sounds strange, but up until a little over a month ago, I had no idea that I was adopted."

Sarah released a heavy breath. He was born in Tahlequah? This gorgeous Californian? No wonder he reminded her of home.

She didn't want to discuss his newly discovered Cherokee roots, but after his personal admission, how could she just get up and walk away? The least she could do was give him a moment of her time, no matter how uncomfortable the subject made her.

"You were adopted by a white family?" she asked.

"Sort of," he answered. "My father was English, but my mom was Spanish and Italian. I always figured my coloring had come from her. You know, all that Latin blood." He glanced down at his drink, then back up. "My parents died when I was in college. They were killed in a plane crash."

"I'm sorry," she whispered. Grief was something that still haunted her. She knew how it could destroy, claw its way into a person's soul. And at this oddly quiet moment, Adam's soul could have been her own. Their gazes were locked much too intimately.

Adam didn't respond. He couldn't. Everything around him had gone still. There was nothing. No one but the woman seated across from him. He wanted to touch her. Make the invisible connection between them more real.

Was it Sarah's eyes that captivated him? Those dark, exotic-shaped eyes? Or was it her hair—the lush black curtain? Her skin was beautiful, too. Clear and smooth and the color of temptation.

Before Adam's imagination took him further, he blinked away his last thought, breaking their stare. Sarah picked up her juice, and he sensed her uneasiness. Was the connection between them loneliness? Was she as alone as he felt? Within the span of a month, everything familiar in Adam's world had changed. He'd moved, switched jobs and stumbled upon his adoption.

"I've been storing some things that belonged to my parents," he said finally. "Mostly personal items, but there were two tall file cabinets from my dad's office. They were filled with old business records, but I kept them anyway." He glanced at Sarah's slender hands, recalling the shock tied to his discovery, the way his own hands had shaken. "I moved recently. Not a major move, just to a place that's closer to work. But since I was reorganizing and packing, it seemed like a good time to clean out those files."

"You found something, didn't you?"

"Yes." He swallowed back the pain, the lump that had formed in his throat. "There was a document from an adoption agency. It was in a manila envelope with some old tax records. I guess that's why I didn't see it before." He swallowed again, then released a heavy breath. "I discovered that

I was born in Tahlequah, Oklahoma, to a Cherokee woman named Cynthia Youngwolf.'' Leaning against the table, he searched Sarah's eyes, hoping for a miracle. "Do you know anyone by that name?''

She shook her head. "Tahlequah is the Cherokee capital. There's a large Indian population there. It would be impossible to know everyone."

Adam's heart sank. "I've been trying to find her, but nothing has panned out. First I checked with the Oklahoma phone directory, and then I placed some personal ads in newspapers. After that, I listed my name with one of those adoption search agencies." He hoped his biological mother was looking for him, too. Looking for the son who had lost his adoptive parents.

Surely Cynthia Youngwolf wondered about him. What woman wouldn't think about the child she had given up?

"This whole thing has been pretty overwhelming."

"I'm sorry I wasn't able to help," Sarah said.

Adam studied her face, features that were strong yet delicate. Vulnerable yet proud. Were other Cherokee women as compelling?

What did his mother look like? And who was his father? Were they secret lovers? Too young to raise a child? He had questions, and no one but Cynthia Youngwolf could answer them.

And what about his parents? The ones who had raised him? Why hadn't they told him that he was adopted?

He couldn't control the turmoil, the jumbled emotions that left him feeling hurt and confused. Why had they lied to him, pretending he was their biological son? They'd had so many opportunities to tell him, especially during all that family counseling.

And what about the critical events leading up to the therapy? Were there subtle hints? Quiet innuendoes? Something, anything that marked the truth?

Yes, he thought, his heart striking his chest. There was.

Adam had been seventeen at the time, a tall, rangy boy with fire in his blood. And two weeks earlier, he'd gotten caught stealing a pint of whiskey from the local market, the place where his mother bought groceries.

Adam had lied, of course, insisting he'd swiped the liquor on a dare. Yet that hadn't stopped his parents from cornering him, from trapping him with one of their mandatory talks. But why? He knew they hadn't found the other bottle, the one he kept hidden in the trunk of his car.

"We picked up some literature," his father said.

Slumped on the couch, Adam glanced up at his dad. His mother sat in nearby chair, twisting the tassel on one of the pillows she'd embroidered. His dad was tense, and his mom was jittery and fretful. Things didn't look good.

"Literature?"

Ronald Paige nodded, a quick, hard jerk of his head. "About alcoholism."

Irritated, he righted his posture. "And what's that got to do with me?"

"You drink, Adam. You drink a lot."

"That's bull." He dragged a hand through his hair and ground a booted heel into the carpet. "I party on the weekends once in a while. That doesn't make me an alcoholic."

"It's more than that, and you know it. You're addicted. All the signs are there."

All the signs are where? he wondered. In some stupid brochure his parents had latched onto? "I'm not going to sit here and listen to this." When he stood, he topped his father by several inches. "You guys are freaking out. Making something out of nothing."

"And you're out of control. You don't even seem like our son anymore."

"Really? Well maybe I wished I wasn't. All you ever do is hassle me." Turning to leave, he caught sight of the look that passed between his parents. A look that said something secretive, something he couldn't quite name.

Shrugging it off, he slammed the front door and headed for his car, grateful the whiskey was still there.

A horn honked and Adam jolted, realizing where he was. He sat in the juice bar, staring blindly out a window. Taking a deep breath, he let it out slowly. He had come a long way since his bout with the bottle, and, up until their untimely death, his parents had remained by his side. The loving, supportive family that had kept his adoption a secret. None of it made sense.

He turned to face Sarah, hoping she could help him unscramble this puzzle. "Do you still have family in Tahlequah? Will you ask them if they've ever heard of Cynthia Youngwolf?"

Her eyes shifted focus. Instead of meeting his gaze, she studied her drink, her tone distant. "My family...my father doesn't live in Tahlequah anymore. He's in another part of Oklahoma now."

"I see," Adam responded, although he didn't. All she would have to do was ask her father about a name, yet she appeared reluctant to do so. Why? he wondered. Why wouldn't she make one simple phone call? And why had her shoulders tensed throughout portions of their conversation?

One minute he saw attraction in her eyes, the next detachment. Warm. Aloof. Gentle. Afraid. She appeared to be all of those things. And that made him want to touch her even more, reach for her hand and hold it. This woman, he thought, this dark-eyed mystery, was connected to his birthplace, a heritage he knew nothing about.

The Cherokee books he'd purchased helped, but they weren't enough. Reading didn't combat the loneliness. He needed more than just words on a page.

He needed human contact.

He needed Sarah.

Adam started. He needed a woman he'd just met? Was he losing his mind? The last of his sanity?

No, he thought. He wasn't crazy. A woman born in Tahlequah, a stunning Cherokee with dark eyes and long, flowing hair. He couldn't have dreamed her if he'd tried. Sarah was the answer he had been waiting for.

She glanced at her watch. "It was nice meeting you, Adam. But I should get back to work."

"I'll walk you," he offered.

They stood on the street corner, and as she brushed his arm, a ray of hope shot through him—an awakening from one of his ancestor's arrows. No, he wasn't about to give up on Sarah Cloud. Somehow, some way, he would break through her defenses, unlock the mystery surrounding her. And in the process, he intended to find his biological mother. The woman who had given him life.

The next week Sarah paced one of the facial rooms, checking and rechecking her supplies. Adam Paige was her next appointment. A facial. The man had booked a facial. Not that she didn't have other male clients. She encouraged men to take better care of their skin, yet the thought of touching Adam made her palms tingle and her pulse race.

She sanitized her hands for the tenth time, a nervous habit, she supposed. And one she'd just acquired. Checking her watch, she exhaled a shaky breath. Maybe he would fall asleep during the facial the way some of her other clients did. It would be easier touching him if he slept.

Sarah let out an anxious laugh. Mrs. Whipple snored during her procedure, but then Vivian Whipple was nearly eighty years old. Young, virile Adam Paige wouldn't snore. And he probably wouldn't fall asleep, either.

Quit stressing and go, she told herself. Adam was probably early, waiting in the reception area for her to greet him.

Sure enough, he was there. As Sarah approached, he stood. Today he wore tan trousers and a matching shirt. Although he looked more stylish than he had the week before, he still exhibited the same rugged appeal. Both the makeup artist and her client checked him out from their vantage point. And, of course, Tina watched with a dreamy smile, probably thinking Sarah was the luckiest girl in L.A.

Yeah, right. More like the most nervous.

"Hi, Adam," Sarah said, reminding herself it was just a facial—a procedure she had done a thousand times before. "Are you ready?"

"Sure. Lead the way."

She showed him where her treatment room was, then took

him to an empty dressing room. "Just remove your shirt and put this on." She handed him a kimono-style robe that belted in front, her friendly, professional voice intact. "And when you're ready, come to the facial room." Pointing to a rack of hangers, she added, "We encourage clients to keep their belongings with them, so be sure to bring your shirt along."

"Okay." He flashed that devastating smile, and she proceeded down the hall, taking a deep, I'll-get-through-this breath. Men might be low on her list of priorities, but this one made her tingly and weak-kneed, sensations she would prefer to do without.

Sarah waited by the treatment chair, resisting the urge to cleanse her hands again. She couldn't wash away her nervousness no matter how hard she tried. Touching Adam was inevitable, and dousing herself with an instant sanitizer wasn't going to help.

When footsteps sounded, she looked up. Adam entered the room, shirt in hand. She took it from him and hung it on a nearby hook. He wore the aqua robe she had given him, and although it was a simple garment, the pale color emphasized every striking feature. She decided his biological parents must have been beautiful, their genes creating a mixed-blood masterpiece.

"Have you ever had a facial before?" she asked.

He smiled again, his teeth white and straight. "No, but I'm looking forward to it."

"Have a seat, and I'll explain the procedure," she said, struggling to focus on her job. She hadn't been this anxious since her state board exam. This jittery inside. How much physical perfection could one man inherit?

He sat on the facial bed, his presence filling the small room. Sarah closed the door, knowing she had to. A relaxed setting enhanced the treatment.

Once she briefed him, he reclined and she draped him with a coverlet. He had chosen to keep the room quiet rather than listen to a CD from Sarah's collection. She had a variety of soft music as well as sounds from nature. She would have preferred to have a CD playing. The silence only made her more aware of her nervousness.

"I'm going to cover your hair," she told him, slipping her hands behind his neck. His hair, banded into a ponytail, felt smooth and thick. Healthy, she thought. Everything about Adam boasted strength.

After analyzing and cleansing his skin, she began the massage. She knew all the clinical benefits of a facial massage, yet when her fingers connected with his skin, she forgot each and every one.

She could have been a woman stroking her lover. A woman exploring his face, the chiseled angles and rawboned sensuality.

Each manipulation felt erotic. Rolling movements, circular friction. She touched his forehead, his cheeks, the bridge of his nose. She allowed her fingers to roam his face, the pressure light but firm, slow yet rhythmic.

Heat against heat, Sarah thought. Flesh against flesh. Adam kept his eyes closed, but he didn't sleep. Instead he moaned his pleasure—a low, masculine sound.

When she accidentally brushed his lips, he wet them afterward. She swallowed and moved down his chin, his neck.

Mesmerized, she became aware of every breath he took, every muscle that twitched, the rise and fall of his chest, the flutter of his eyelids.

He made another low sound and shifted his weight, causing the coverlet to slip. The V on his robe gaped. Sarah was tempted to slide her hands inside, massage his chest, his nipples.

Catching her breath, she chastised herself. She had to end this now. What kind of esthetician fantasized about her client? A stranger?

A beautiful stranger.

Easing back as naturally as possible, she broke contact, lifting her hands to fill a basin with warm water.

Adam opened his eyes, blinking as though awakening from a dream. He tilted his head back and looked at Sarah.

"That was nice," he said, his voice a husky whisper.

She managed a shaky smile, uncertain of how to respond. Her fingertips still tingled, and the gaping robe still exposed his chest—gorgeous, golden-brown flesh. She even caught sight of a taut, muscular belly.

Sarah adjusted the coverlet, knowing it was her professional place to do so. Adam didn't seem to notice that his robe had slipped open, but then why would he? Most men bared their chests without modesty.

"I'm going to remove the moisturizer, then prepare a mask," she told him, an image of his navel imbedded in her mind.

She continued the procedure, shielding his eyes with moist cotton pads. They didn't talk while she applied the mask, and within an hour the treatment was complete, his skin firm and clean.

He stood and smoothed his hair, his robe still loose, the belt barely tied. "Thank you, Sarah," he said, coming forward to press some folded bills into her hand.

"You're welcome." She accepted the tip, realizing they were only inches apart. He wasn't wearing cologne, she thought, her heart fluttering in her breast. He smelled natural, like fresh-milled soap.

"Will you have dinner with me tonight?"

The invitation caught her by surprise. And so did her response. Without the slightest hesitation, Sarah agreed to share a meal with him—this tall, beautiful stranger. A man she knew she should avoid.

Adam stood in the main square of Chinatown, waiting for his date. This was insane, he thought. No matter how hard he'd tried, he hadn't been able to convince Sarah to allow him to pick her up at her apartment. She had insisted on meeting him.

He checked his watch. 7:20 p.m. She was late. Was he about to be stood up? It would serve him right, he supposed. Plenty of women chased him, and he'd gotten used to the attention. But then, that attention was based on his looks, not on the man he was inside. And he wanted more than a superficial relationship. He wanted…

What? A commitment?

Someday, maybe. But he wasn't looking for love. At least not at this time in his life. He had too many other issues, too many other goals—like finding his biological mother, bonding with his heritage. He couldn't think about love and commitment. Not until he knew who he was and where he had come from.

He released a heavy breath. So where did Sarah fit into this? Why was he so eager to see her again?

Because she fascinated him, he realized. And she could lead him to his roots. Adam knew he was lost, a ship that needed to come to port. The adoption had him feeling so damn disconnected. For the past month he had been floating. Going nowhere.

And he had the same vibe about Sarah. He suspected she was troubled, too. And that drew him to her, made him want to help. She was solid, real—so unlike the superficial women who chased him. She would make a good friend.

A good friend? he asked himself. Or a compatible lover? He couldn't very well deny the sexual spark between them. He hadn't counted on it, but it was there—lurking, hiding, waiting to be released.

Well he wasn't about to release it. The last thing he needed was to complicate a new friendship with sex. He would just have to keep those urges under control.

And just how was he supposed to do that? He had already booked another facial for next week. He wanted her to stroke him again, enchant him with her magic.

Her mystery.

Adam frowned. Already his hormones were interfering with a friendship that hadn't even happened yet. He could find another connection to his heritage, couldn't he? He didn't need Sarah to show him the way.

A beautiful, exotic woman. A dark-eyed Cherokee mystery.

Damn. Maybe he should just forget the friendship and have

an affair with her. A passionate one-night stand. That would satisfy his hormones, the unexpected lust.

Disturbed by the thought, he shook his head. Maybe it would be better if Sarah did stand him up. Then he wouldn't have to worry about their attraction.

Adam checked his watch again, then glanced up and caught his breath. It was too late, he thought. Much too late.

Beautiful, dark-eyed Sarah was already walking toward him, and all he could think about was tangling his hands in all that glorious hair and kissing her senseless.

Two

Sarah scanned the menu, wishing she could think of something to say. She wasn't good at small talk and was even worse at dating. How was she supposed to concentrate on what to order with Adam sitting across from her? A man who appeared relaxed and confident? He probably had the dating ritual down pat.

She stole a quick glance. Of course he did. Look at him. God's gift to womankind. He wore his hair in a ponytail, his clothes casual but trendy—a printed shirt and pre-washed jeans sporting a well-known label. California ranch wear, she decided, designed for the city cowboy. His rugged style appeared natural. He didn't try to attract attention. He just did.

He caught her eye, and she looked down, studied her hands. "Did you know that they don't serve fortune cookies in China?"

She glanced up again, forcing herself to hold his gaze. "Why not?"

"They were invented in the U.S. They don't exist in China."

"Have you been there?"

"No. I read that on the Internet in a travel guide. I spend a lot of time online."

Sarah took a deep breath, told herself she would get through this date. It helped not thinking of him as a world traveler. She had never even been on a plane. "I'm glad they serve them here. Fortune cookies are my favorite part of a Chinese meal."

He smiled. "Me, too."

When his smile faded, their eyes met. They sat in a small red booth, candlelight flickering between them. His face fascinated her, but she had already touched it, explored the ridges and angles, the masculine texture of his skin. She didn't want to remember every detail, but looking at him made that impossible.

He lifted the teapot and offered her a refill. She shook her head. She hadn't finished the first cup yet.

"Let's choose a few extra entrées so we can share," he said.

"All right." She agreed even though the suggestion sounded oddly intimate. "I would prefer chicken and vegetables, though. I don't eat red meat."

He smiled at her, something he did often, she noticed.

"Me, neither," he said, his voice as easy as his smile. "I guess that means we're going to get along just fine."

Yes, she thought, if she could just get over her nervousness, tame the unwelcome flutter in her stomach.

When the waiter arrived, they ordered a variety of dishes. Adam spoke a little Cantonese, enough to surprise Sarah and please the grinning waiter. Sarah wondered if Adam had learned the language on the Internet. He appeared to know a lot more than just the history of fortune cookies.

"Ancient cultures fascinate me," he told her. "I had some training in traditional Chinese medicine. It's an integral part of their philosophy and religion. Much like the Native American culture." He lifted his tea. "I've been reading about the Cherokee."

Sarah frowned. She didn't want to discuss her heritage.

And coming from Adam, the term *Native American* sounded almost glamorous. A far cry from her roots. She was just a simple Indian girl from Oklahoma.

"Where did you get your formal training?" she asked, hoping to steer clear of Cherokee subjects.

"First I attended a school of herbal studies in Northern California, then transferred to a university in London"

"London? You went to school in England?" Maybe he was more of a world traveler than she had originally thought. "Did you like living there?"

"Sure. It's a beautiful country, and the University of Westminster was an excellent school."

His casual response made her feel even more Indian, and she hated the feeling. Adam's adoptive mother might have been Latino, but he'd been raised in a predominantly white world. Apparently his brown skin hadn't hindered his experiences. "It sounds exciting, but expensive, too."

"My dad was an accountant, one of those conservative guys who saved money for his son's education. We weren't rich, but I didn't go without, either."

His adoptive father must have been an honorable man, she thought with a twinge of admiration and a sting of envy. Sarah's father hadn't saved a dime. She had struggled to pay for her own schooling.

Their dinner arrived, and they ate in silence, his gaze catching hers between bites. Feeling shy, she glanced away. His mouth fascinated her. The way he moistened his lips before he lifted the fork.

He leaned toward her, and suddenly, foolishly, she wished the table wasn't between them.

"Sarah?"

"Yes?"

"Are you enjoying your meal?"

She nodded, even though her stomach was still alive with nerves, the flutter of feminine anxiety. "Yes. It's quite good."

He smiled, and she took a deep breath, recalling the warmth of his skin.

* * *

Night settled in the sky, scattering stars around a quarter moon. Adam and Sarah walked through the Chinatown courtyard, strolling in and out of boutiques. Adam loved the area. A few of the vendors knew him by name. He spent a lot of time in Chinatown, purchasing herbs and admiring the culture.

He turned to look at Sarah. As many times as he came here, he had never brought a date. Not until today.

She smiled a little shyly, and he considered holding her hand. Then reconsidered when she clutched her purse strap with the hand closest to his. There was no point in pushing too hard. If something developed between them, it would happen naturally.

"Have you been to Chinatown before?" he asked.

"Once, when I first moved here."

"And when was that?"

"Six years ago. I was eighteen at the time."

Adam nodded. He could almost see her, fresh out of high school—a little Oklahoma girl heading for the golden state. She was still little, he realized. Small and feminine in a way that made him yearn to protect her. But whether or not she would welcome protection, he couldn't be sure. In spite of her petite frame, independence shone through. She didn't have to tell him that she had ventured to California alone.

Independent yet vulnerable. Suddenly Adam was reminded of the stray cats that came to his door, the smooth, sleek creatures he couldn't seem to resist. He gave them their space, but he fed them, too. And those scouting a cozy place to sleep inevitably found their way into his bed.

Adam looked at Sarah again, wondering if she would find her way into his bed. If she would nuzzle and purr, arch and stretch against him. A smooth, sleek creature he wouldn't be able to resist.

Frowning, he shook his head. She wasn't a lost kitten. And he was thinking with his libido, creating sexual scenarios on a first date. So much for not pushing too hard.

"What's your favorite thing about California?" he asked, forcing himself to clear his mind.

She stopped to gaze at a window display. "That's easy." Turning toward him, she smiled. "The beaches. I love the sand and the surf. I like to go there at dusk, when it's quiet."

She sighed, and Adam pictured her at the beach on a windy day, dressed in an oversize sweater and jeans, her waist-length hair blowing in the breeze. "You collect shells, don't you?"

She widened her eyes. "Yes. How did you know?"

Because he could see her walking along the shore, shells glinting in her hand like pieces of eight. She was, he decided, a woman who appreciated simple treasures. "A good guess, I suppose. Do you want to check out this shop?"

"Sure."

They entered the boutique and scanned the crammed interior. It held a collection of goods, many of them jewelry and trinkets, shiny items meant to attract a woman's eye. Sarah looked around, then wandered over to a small circular rack of clothing. Intrigued, Adam watched her.

She admired a satin dress, tilting her head as she stroked the shiny red fabric.

"It's pretty," Adam said, noting the traditional mandarin collar and intricate embroidered design.

"Yes." Her voice held a note of feminine awe.

The proprietor, a tiny Chinese woman offering a friendly smile, walked over to them. She was old, Adam thought, ancient and charming. She patted Sarah's shoulder with a gnarled hand.

"You try on," she said, her accent making her English choppy.

Sarah turned, hugged the garment in a startled reaction. "Oh, no. Thank you, though."

"We have a private fitting room." The woman pointed to a corner where an ornate brass rod housed a silky green drape.

"I'm just browsing." Sarah replaced the dress, giving it one last glance.

The old woman said, "Okay," then headed toward the front counter.

Perplexed, Adam studied his date. She had looked at the garment with longing, yet refused to indulge herself. Sarah Cloud was a mystery, a dark-eyed princess who wore plain clothes and collected seashells at dusk. He didn't know how to pursue her, wasn't sure if he should try. She confused as much as fascinated him.

"Why didn't you try the dress on?" he asked.

She crossed her arms in what seemed like a protective, if not slightly defiant gesture. "It's too fancy."

"I think it's perfect."

"Not for me."

Did everyone see her beauty but her? he wondered. Most beautiful women in L.A. were used to attention, yet Sarah didn't appear to notice an appreciative eye. Of course she wasn't from California, he reminded himself. And that alone appealed to him. Since he'd lost his parents, the City of Angels and everything it represented no longer felt right. But in spite of his European education, it was all he knew.

Sarah had asked him about England, and he had tried to respond as casually as possible. His parents had died while he was in London. He had come home to bury them, then returned to finish his studies, knowing his career was all he had left. But that hadn't been something he could discuss over dinner, not on a first date, not when he'd wanted to keep the evening light. And there was nothing light about the death of his parents—the caring, supportive family that had lied to him. It hurt so badly, sometimes he couldn't breathe.

Adam looked at Sarah and noticed her arms were still crossed. She was tense, but suddenly so was he. "Let's buy something," he said, hoping to ease the tension. "You pick out a souvenir for me, and I'll choose one for you."

"You're kidding, right?"

"Nope." And he intended to con her into the red dress. "Come on." He led her to the other side of the store. "Find something you think I'd like."

Baffled, Sarah wandered through the tiny boutique. She didn't know what to choose for Adam. She wasn't an experienced shopper. And the only items she collected came from the sea. She didn't buy shells; she lifted them from the sand, even broken and chipped ones.

He smiled at her, and her stomach unleashed a flurry of wings. Beautiful butterflies, she decided. It wasn't nerves this time. It was the flutter of attraction.

Curious about his upbringing, she wanted to ask him about his mother and why he was determined to replace her with the woman who had given him up. But she decided now wasn't the time for that sort of conversation.

Maybe she was curious about Adam's mother because she missed her own. Sarah didn't have anything to remember her mother by, no outdated dresses, no feminine little keepsakes. Her father had burned everything. But that had been part of their culture, the old Cherokee way. A path she no longer followed.

Sarah looked up at Adam. He watched her. Closely. Maybe too closely. Before he could ask what she had been thinking about, she returned to the business at hand. She still had to find him a souvenir.

Scanning the shelves, she caught sight of a teapot. But not just any teapot. This one was adorned with a hand-painted dragon. The serpent's body shimmered with gold, and its eyes were set with shiny red stones. Yes, she thought, a powerful creature spun from legend. A man like Adam would slay this beast, assume the role of the protective knight, the fairy-tale prince.

She lifted it, turned it in her hand. The serpent's eyes shined back at her. The detail was exquisite. The dragon seemed alive, ready to breathe a burst of iridescent flames. She could almost feel the heat. The scorch of fire.

"This," she said. "Do you like it?"

Adam blinked. "It's a teapot, Sarah."

"It has a dragon on it," she pointed out.

"Yeah, but it's still a teapot."

She stifled a smile. He looked as if she had just squelched his masculinity. "You drink tea, so what's wrong with a teapot?"

"Nothing, I guess. It's just not what I figured you'd choose."

She touched the serpent. "I think he's dangerous." Like the way Adam made her feel. Suddenly she was caught up in the moment, in the fairy tale she had created in her mind.

Adam studied the teapot, and the winged flutter erupted in her stomach again. And when he took a small step toward her, the motion intensified.

"Okay. I'll take the dragon," he said. "But I want you to try on that dress."

Her heartbeat jumped. "Why?"

"Because I want to see you in it."

"It won't look right on me," she said, feeling suddenly foolish. "I'm not a red satin kind of girl." She wore mostly pastels, simple skirts and blouses constructed of washable fabrics. Never red. And never satin.

"You'll never know until you try it on."

Was he challenging her? Baiting her? Either way, she knew she had to prove him wrong. Sarah considered herself a practical woman. She had no use for such a luxurious garment. It wouldn't fit her looks or her lifestyle.

"Fine. I'll try it on." She turned and headed toward the clothing rack, knowing Adam followed. Retrieving the dress, she darted into the fitting room without glancing back.

She closed the curtain, removed her wedged sandals and unbuttoned her blouse. Slipping off her skirt, she eyed the dress. It looked much too bright next to her mint green ensemble. The dress zipped in back, so she peeled it open and stepped into the opening. The moment the fabric touched her skin, she shivered. It felt cool. Slick. Almost wet.

Fighting those sensations, she forced herself to continue. She couldn't reach the zipper to close it all the way, nor could she attach the tiny hooks that fastened behind the collar. She fumbled with them, then gave up and studied herself.

The woman in the mirror startled her. Nothing about the image seemed familiar. Her waist-length hair spilled over red satin, like onyx melting over rubies—jewels from the fairy tale she had created. Tilting her head, she ran her hands over her body. Even with the zipper partially undone, the dress molded to her curves.

Decadent. Sensual.

Wrong, she told herself, suddenly nervous. This wasn't her.

With a pounding heart, she fastened her sandals and emerged from the fitting room. She would prove to Adam the dress wasn't right. She would…

…slam into his gaze and lose her breath.

He stood tall and handsome, watching her, his stare bewitching. The knight. The fairy-tale prince. The dragon slayer.

"I told you it was too fancy," she said.

"No," he countered quietly. "It's perfect. Let me buy it for you."

She shook her head, but he persisted. "Wear it now, Sarah. Wear it for me."

How in God's name could she refuse? Deny the husky pleasure in his voice?

Realizing the zipper was still undone, she chewed her lip. "I…um…couldn't zip it all the way. Will you ask the saleslady to help me?"

He smiled. "Does that mean you're going to let me buy it for you?"

She nodded. "Yes. Thank you. I've never owned anything like this before."

Adam moved closer. "I can zip it for you."

No, she thought. Her heart was already thumping against her ribs. And her stomach. That wild winged flutter. "But it has these tiny hooks." She placed her hand on the back of her neck, trying to explain, trying to keep him from coming any closer.

His smile turned boyish. "I think I can manage."

He didn't give her a choice. He approached her, so she turned around. How many women had he dressed? she wondered. Or undressed?

"Lift your hair," he said, his voice quiet once again.

Decadent. Sleek. Dangerous. The words spun in her head, making her dizzy.

She pulled her hair to one side, felt him touch her. His hands were deft, steady and controlled.

He zipped the dress, then went after the hooks, his breath brushing her nape. A shiver raced up her spine, but she wasn't cold. She was warm. Much too warm.

"All done."

"Thank you."

She turned and found herself inches from him.

He moistened his lips, and she swallowed. Was he going to kiss her? She wanted him to, yet she couldn't imagine letting it happen. Not here. Not in this tiny boutique. There were other customers, and the saleslady watched them from behind the counter.

Sarah stepped back and lifted her arm where the price tag dangled. "This needs to be cut."

He nodded, but didn't say anything. He was staring at her. Fixated, it seemed, on her mouth. Finally, he blinked and smiled.

Still a little dizzy, she returned his smile, and they walked to the front counter. He paid for his purchase with a credit card. She with cash. The old woman removed the tag on the dress and packed the teapot in a sturdy box. Sarah, wrapped gloriously in red satin, accepted a shopping bag with her old clothes folded inside.

They stepped into the night air, and she filled her lungs, chasing away the dizziness. An array of buildings surrounded them, a blend of ancient architecture and modern accents.

"Where did you learn to speak Cantonese?" she asked Adam, as he guided her toward a secluded bench.

"From coming here and talking to the people." He placed his package on the ground and waited for Sarah to sit. "But I only know conversational phrases. Languages aren't easy to grasp unless you use them all the time."

She nodded. She only remembered bits and pieces of the Cherokee dialect, words her mother had spoken. But that seemed like a lifetime ago.

They sat quietly, stars glittering in the sky, a small breeze cooling the summer air. Sarah enjoyed the silence until

Adam's gaze became too intense. She shifted a little, uncrossed her legs, then crossed them again, unsure of what to do with herself. The dizziness returned—the shaky, wild, fluttery sensation.

She looked away, pretended to study a building, her pulse racing.

Would sex make her feel this way? she wondered. Hot and hungry? Excited yet nervous? Sarah was a virgin—a woman who still lived in the shadow of an old-fashioned upbringing, keeping herself pure for love.

Or was that a lie? she asked herself. Was she saving herself for the right man? Or using her virginity as an excuse to protect her heart?

"What are you thinking about?"

Adam's question startled her. "Nothing important," she responded, knowing she couldn't tell him where her mind had wandered.

"I was thinking about dragons," he said.

"What about them?"

His voice turned quiet, a little husky. "The embroidery on your dress. I didn't realize it before, but it's a dragon."

"It is?" She glanced down, saw the image come suddenly to life. What had looked like an intricate pattern was actually a gold serpent twining around her breasts, her tummy, her hips. And Adam's gaze followed every curve, desire flashing in his eyes.

She couldn't stop what was happening, nor did she want to. They moved in perfect harmony. Synchronized, slow— dancers coming together at the same moment. She wet her lips. He slid his hands into her hair. She made a kittenish sound, and he kissed her.

Pleasure caught at the back of her throat, then flowed through every vein, every cell, every muscle. She grew hot. Needy. Her flesh burned, her nipples ignited. She wanted him to caress her, slay the dragon scorching her body.

He did. He touched, stroked, ran those clever hands over the fire. She had never felt so helpless, yet so completely alive. A smoldering kiss in public. It wasn't proper, but God help her, she didn't care.

They were in their own world, and nothing could penetrate it but passion. His tongue swept her mouth—a mating—over and over. The motion was sexual. And that was what she wanted.

She had needs, strong, overwhelming needs. She wouldn't lose her heart. Sex wasn't love. She could sleep with him tonight.

Sleep with him? Was that what she wanted? To lose her virginity to a man she barely knew? A man obsessed with his newly discovered Cherokee roots? A man romanticizing the culture she'd left behind?

Her head reeling, Sarah pulled away from Adam's kiss.

He made her flesh tingle, her heartbeat accelerate, but she couldn't be with him. No matter what her mother had said, modern warriors didn't exist. And neither did dragon slayers.

"Sarah, what's wrong?"

"I think it's time for me to go," she responded, clasping her nervous hands in her lap. She needed to escape this moment, the spicy taste of his kiss still lingering on her tongue.

"But why? Tell me what's wrong."

"Nothing. I just want to go home." She stood, lifted her purse. She couldn't explain, couldn't ease his conscience. He hadn't offended her. He had aroused her, made her feel too good.

He rose from the bench, his gaze searching hers for the answer she refused to give. "I'll walk you to your car."

"Honestly, Adam. I'll be fine. Thank you for dinner. For the dress." Something she should have never accepted. Gathering the bag of her old clothes, she left him standing at the bench, Chinatown dazzling around him.

Three

A week passed, and Adam still battled his emotions. His work day had ended, but he sat in the conference room at the clinic, checking his watch. Then rechecking it. In twenty minutes, he had an appointment with Sarah. He hadn't spoken to her since their date, and he'd expected her to reschedule his facial, refer him to another esthetician. But she hadn't done that.

Of course not. She was too professional to turn away a client, to let personal feelings interfere with her job.

And what exactly were her feelings? he wondered. To him, their kiss had seemed so right, so naturally erotic, especially when she'd made those sexy little sounds. Like a stray kitten, he thought, mewling in satisfaction. Now that damn fantasy wouldn't go away.

Maybe she didn't want to be the object of his desire, the woman he lusted after. Adam frowned. Had he really put his hands all over her? Yeah, he had. And even though he longed to do it again, he still owed her an apology. That kiss had been a little too wild, too hungry for public display.

An apology would set things right. They could be friends, couldn't they? They didn't have to get romantically involved. He could lay his urges to rest, but he couldn't let Sarah go. Not completely.

He was too caught in the mystery surrounding her. Why was she hiding from her heritage? What could have possibly happened to turn her away from her roots? Adam needed to know. Being Cherokee was their link, a bond he hoped to strengthen.

He left the clinic and entered the salon. The blond receptionist grinned when she saw him. He returned her smile, but just as he approached the desk, he spotted Sarah coming around the corner.

The blonde spoke up first. "Sarah, your five o'clock is here."

"Thank you, Tina," she responded, shifting her gaze to Adam.

He walked toward her, and she slipped her hands in her pockets. She wore a white lab coat over her clothes, but it didn't make her look clinical. Instead she looked pure—a dark-haired, dark-eyed angel.

"Hi," he said.

"Hi," she repeated, her voice fighting a strained note. "Go ahead and change, and I'll meet you in the treatment room."

"Okay." He knew the receptionist was watching, and he knew it made Sarah even more uncomfortable than she already was. He should cancel the facial, let her off the hook, but he needed some quiet time with her, to apologize without an audience.

Five minutes later, he entered the treatment room, shirt in hand. He hung it on a nearby hook and waited for Sarah to acknowledge him. She was still setting up, filling disposable containers with creams and lotions.

She turned, and their eyes met. Silence, still and awkward, engulfed the room. Neither spoke. Adam became aware of everything—the pounding of his heart beneath the robe, the hitch in Sarah's breath, the way her hands shook.

He had no right to put her through this. He had to ease the

tension. Walking toward her, he managed a smile, even though his heart picked up speed. Being near her did that to him, he realized. And it wasn't a comforting thought, trying to calm a woman when he wasn't particularly stable himself.

Sensuality sizzled between them. Nervous and edgy, maybe. But it was there, a thickness in the air he couldn't deny. Couldn't control.

"Let me help," he said, reaching for one of the disposable containers.

"No, it's okay, I can…"

Their fingers brushed, an innocent touch that sent shock waves through his unstable heart, his yearning body.

Sarah must have felt it, too. She pulled back, knocking over a nearby jar. It rolled onto the floor, spilling a citrus-scented lotion.

"Damn it." Her voice shook as badly as her hands. She dashed over to the paper-towel dispenser and tore one in her haste. "I can't seem to do anything right today."

Because of me, Adam thought. Because their attraction was so intense.

She knelt on the floor and began soaking up the mess. He lowered himself beside her. "It was my fault," he said, taking the paper towels away from her. "I startled you."

"It was an accident." Avoiding eye contact, she released an audible breath. "I'll get something to clean up the residue." She went to a cabinet and returned with a spray cleanser and another wad of paper towels.

They worked side by side, concentrating on the task at hand. They didn't look at each other, didn't speak. Instead they gazed at the vinyl floor as if the pattern held great importance.

"I think we should cancel the facial," he said, when the overwhelming silence became too much to bear.

"I think so, too." She sat back on her heels. "I'm just not myself today. I almost called in sick."

Which said it all, he thought. She had been anxiety-ridden about seeing him, enough to make herself ill. His apology was long overdue.

"Sarah, I'm sorry. I didn't mean to get carried away last week. I shouldn't have kissed you the way I did. And certainly not in public."

She twisted a dry paper towel. "I...um...we both got carried away. It wasn't all your fault."

"Then why don't we start over?" He stood and offered her a hand, trying to keep his voice casual, his heartbeat steady.

She accepted his hand, but let go the moment she was on her feet. Leaning over, she picked up the soiled paper towels, then tossed them into the wastebasket. "I don't think we should go out again. I don't think it would work."

"I meant as friends." He tried not to frown. The rejection stung, even if he had been prepared for it. "I know you're not comfortable dating me. But I think we have a lot in common, and I'd like to be friends."

She sent him a small smile. "That's a nice thing to say."

"Then you're willing to start over?"

Sarah nodded, although a part of her could still taste his kiss, feel the heat of his body next to hers. Struggling with the image, she sanitized her hands, wringing them together. In spite of their attraction, friendship was best. Dating Adam was out of the question.

Why? she asked herself. Why was she going to deprive herself of his kiss, his touch?

Because it might lead to sex, a step she wasn't ready to take. How could she become intimate with a man obsessed with finding his Cherokee family when she had left her own behind? And then, of course, there was her virginity. She couldn't pretend that her moral upbringing didn't matter. She had made a promise to her mother. And she couldn't forget that youthful vow.

Don't give yourself to a man unless he's special to you, unless you love him.

But how will I know the difference?

You'll know, sweet Sarah. You'll know.

She could see herself sitting on the edge of a lace-draped bed, gazing at her mother, her head filled with wonder. It could have been yesterday. Or it could have been a lifetime ago. A dreamy twelve-year-old girl who had just experienced her first menstrual cycle.

I'll wait for the right man, Mom. I promise.

She blinked, looked at Adam and noticed how stunning he was—the planes and angles of his face, the broad shoulders, slim hips. And his smile, that warm, genuine smile.

Yes, he was handsome, but she wouldn't fool herself into believing he was the right man.

"Sarah?"

"Yes?"

"Will you have dinner with me tomorrow night?" He held up a hand as if to fend off an expected protest. "A friendship dinner at my house. Just a casual meal." He flashed that devastating smile. "What do you say?"

"You're offering to cook for me?"

"Well, sort of." His grin turned a little sheepish. "I'll probably just throw some sandwiches together. Maybe a salad."

Sarah laughed. "How can a guy who eats health food not know how to cook?"

"Oh, I don't know. He lives on veggie burgers. The frozen kind you pop in the microwave." He smiled at her again. "So, will you come over tomorrow night? Suffer through one of my bland meals?"

"Yes," she said, charmed by his honesty. Besides, she thought, curiosity had gotten the best of her. She couldn't help but wonder where he lived.

He lived in a guest house in Sherman Oaks, not too far from Sarah's apartment. She smoothed her blouse, then knocked on the door. She had actually stressed about what to wear, then decided on jeans and a plain blue top. Everything she owned was simple, she supposed. Everything but the red satin dress.

Adam opened the door and stunned her senses. Classic rock played on the stereo, and his jeans were faded, the knees fraying just a little. She heard a loud "meow" and watched a black cat brush her leg as it darted past.

"Hey, Sarah. Come on in. Don't worry about Darrin," he added, apparently referring to the cat, "he's allowed to go out."

Sarah entered the house and took in her surroundings—hardwood floors, heavy oak furniture and tall, leafy plants in every corner.

The clean, masculine decor suited him. As always, Adam wore his long hair secured in a ponytail.

Handing him a small packet, she said, "It's fresh honey. For your tea. I didn't know what else to bring."

"Thanks. I guess you're not going to let me forget about that teapot, are you?"

"What?" She blinked and realized he was teasing her. "You're an herbalist. You're supposed to brew your own tea."

She gave a start when something moved. Another cat, she told herself foolishly as a furry being pounced onto the back of the sofa. This one was white with big curious eyes.

"How many cats to do you have?" she inquired, petting the friendly creature.

"There's usually five or six around here. Most of them are strays, so the number changes. Some just visit and others have decided to stay. Cameo is a permanent resident. She's expecting a litter soon." He nodded to the sturdy feline. "She showed up at my door pregnant. There wasn't much I could do."

But spoil her, Sarah supposed. Cameo looked pampered and well loved.

"Dinner won't be long," Adam said. "I was in the middle of fixing the salad, and the spaghetti is almost done."

"Spaghetti? I thought we were having sandwiches."

He shrugged. "I figured boiling some water and opening a jar of sauce wouldn't be too hard."

She laughed. "Can I help with anything?"

"Sure. The table still needs to be set."

His roomy kitchen displayed a garden window filled with

potted herbs. The appliances were white, the butcher-block table just big enough for two. She hung her purse on the back of a chair and inhaled the cooking aroma. Apparently he'd added fresh oregano to the store-bought sauce.

"Dinner smells wonderful."

"I'm figuring it out." He smiled. "Would you like something to drink? Water? Milk? Juice?"

His beverage selection pleased her and so did the fact that she didn't see a bottle of wine breathing on the counter. She avoided alcohol, even with dinner. "No thanks, I'm fine."

The CD on the stereo shifted from classic rock to vintage country, and she realized his taste in music was as diverse as her own. Stray cats and eclectic songs. She couldn't help but like him.

He pointed out the appropriate cabinets and drawers, and she set the table, feeling surprisingly relaxed. His plates and bowls were heavy stoneware, his silverware stamped with a geometric pattern. She turned and spotted the dragon sitting on a cluttered oak shelf. Its jeweled eyes glowed back at her.

Adam removed the pasta from the stove and dumped it into a large serving bowl.

And then he winked, jarring her composure with a perfect white smile. She had to tell her woman's heart to behave. It flipped in her chest, forcing her to catch her breath. He was just too handsome for his own good.

"Dinner's ready, sweet Sarah."

Sweet Sarah. Stunned, she stared at him, her jittery heart flooding with emotion. Her mother used to call her that.

"Lemon?"

"I'm sorry, what?"

"Do you want lemon?" He poured her a glass of carbonated water, held it up.

"Yes, thank you." She told herself it was coincidence. It didn't mean anything. He didn't know about her nickname, didn't know that it made her ache for childhood dreams and fairy-tale wishes. The beauty her father had destroyed.

They sat across from each other, a ceiling fan turning slowly overhead.

Refusing to focus on her jumbled emotions, Sarah started a conversation. "Didn't you just move into this house about a month ago?"

Adam nodded. "About the same time I started working at the clinic. Regardless, I'm due for a vacation. I haven't had any time off in years."

"So did they agree to give you some time off even though you're new?"

"Yeah. A couple of weeks in August."

"I was thinking about taking a vacation this summer, too. Sleep in and be lazy. Sometimes it feels good to do nothing." She placed her napkin on her lap. "So what made you decide to switch jobs anyway?"

"The new facility has more to offer. There's a yoga studio and a natural pharmacy in the building. There's also a masseuse and a variety of practitioners." He poured dressing on his salad, then glanced up. "I would love to open a wellness center someday. Of course, there are some things I would do differently."

Sarah understood. She often thought of opening her own skin-care salon. She tasted the spaghetti, alternating bites between her salad.

"Adam, why is it so important for you to find your biological mother? Why would you want to replace your parents with the woman who gave you up?"

"I never said I was trying to replace them. But damn it, I don't understand why they didn't tell me that I was adopted."

So he was hurt, she thought. And confused. "Maybe they were protecting you."

He made a face. "From what? Come on, Sarah. I had the right to know."

She sighed. "I hate to say this, but there's a good chance that your biological mother won't want to see you. She might feel as though you're interfering in her life."

He lifted his water, took a sip. "Then that's a chance I'll have to take. Besides, I think most women give up their babies because they're unable to care for them, not because they don't want them."

"It was a closed adoption."

"That doesn't mean anything. My mom could have been forced to give me up. She could have been too young or too poor. Or it could have been one of those tragic-type love stories. It's obvious my father was white. Maybe the difference in their cultures kept them apart." He reached for a breadstick, dipped it into a bowl of marinara sauce. "I'm not going to quit searching. After I find my mom, I'm going to look for my dad. I want to know both of them."

Sarah shook her head. Did he have foolish notions about reuniting his parents? Bringing lost lovers back together?

"You're still skeptical," he said.

She shrugged. "It's my nature, I suppose."

"But you would probably do the same thing if you were in my situation. Uncovering the circumstances of my birth will fill a void in my life. I'm part Cherokee, Sarah. I belong to a nation of people I know nothing about."

"Maybe your biological mother didn't want you to be raised by an Indian family."

"That's possible, I suppose. But if that's the way she felt, then I need to know why. Don't you think I have a right to know about my culture, learn everything I can?" He paused, pointed to the plants crowding the window sill. "I've devoted most of my adult life to alternative medicine, but that didn't come from the way I was raised. My adoptive mom grew herbs for cooking purposes, but I took it a step further. I studied about their healing properties on my own. Isn't it possible that's the Cherokee in me?" He met her gaze, his voice taking on a wistful tone. "Maybe there was a medicine man in my family."

Sarah sighed. She respected the healer in Adam, but he was caught up in the Indian mystique, glorifying it in a way that would only lead to disappointment. She knew firsthand that the old ways were lost. Her father was living proof of the Cherokee lifestyle today—false promises and alcoholism. There wasn't a medicine man on earth who could take away the pain William Cloud had caused.

When the opportunity arose, Sarah changed the topic of

conversation. She didn't want to talk about being Cherokee, didn't want to think about it or relive it in her mind.

After dinner, Adam and Sarah sat on the patio, the sky sprinkled with stars, the summer air cooled by a soft, intermittent breeze. Adam admired his companion, thinking how beautiful she looked—her hair a long, luxurious curtain, her eyes as dark and mysterious as the night. No wonder she had come to the City of Angels. She was one of them, he thought. A lost angel.

Something was wrong in her life, and he wanted to fix it, make her pain go away.

"Do you eat sweets anymore?" she asked.

Adam quirked an eyebrow. Her question seemed out of the blue, but everything about Sarah Cloud was unpredictable. "No. At least I haven't in a long time."

"Me, neither. But don't you ever want to cheat?"

He couldn't help but smile. "Yeah. Every once in a while I get a craving."

"Me, too. Chocolate eclairs are my favorite. I love the custard filling."

She made a hungry little moaning sound, and Adam pictured her mouth sinking into the rich, creamy pastry. Damn it. Now he wanted to touch her, slide his arms around her waist, ease his body next to hers, slip his tongue...

He studied her lips, the full, alluring shape. Kissing wasn't an option. He had agreed to friendship. No romantic entanglement.

Then why couldn't he convince his hormones of that?

He sipped his tea, hoping the honey-flavored brew would ease his craving, give his mouth something to do. The taste of her, the fevered flavor of their forbidden kiss, still lingered in his mind.

"Do you want to cheat next time?" he asked.

Her voice turned soft. "Are we talking about dessert?"

"Yes," he responded. "We won't be so guilty if we do it together."

She looked at him from across the table, and like magnets

drawn to metal, their gazes locked and held. Sarah pushed her hair off her shoulder, and Adam gripped the handle on his cup. They could move, make unimportant gestures, but they couldn't take their eyes off each other. Couldn't stop staring.

Suddenly the world around them ceased, sounds and scents fading. She felt it, too, he thought. The sexual pull. The heat that wasn't supposed to happen. They weren't talking about chocolate eclairs.

"I don't think cheating is a good idea," she said, breaking their unnerving stare.

"Yeah," he agreed, his voice huskier than usual. "We have more discipline than that."

She folded her hands on her lap. "Of course we do."

They sat quietly then, and Adam noticed the world had returned. The breeze blew a little stronger, stirring scents from his garden. He turned toward the plants and studied the small crop, needing to focus on something other than the attraction he had vowed to ignore.

"I read that when traditional Cherokees gather wild herbs, they ask a plant for its permission to be gathered, then leave a small gift of thanks," he said, thinking it was a beautiful practice. He wondered how it would feel to leave a shining bead on the ground in place of a plant.

"Was that in one of your text books?" she asked.

He shook his head. "I subscribe to a Cherokee newspaper. I get it online, in digest form, and they post cultural tidbits in every issue. Unfortunately my education didn't include Native American practices, at least not to any degree."

"The elders pass along things like that."

"I don't know any elders," he said, watching her tight expression, the one that came over her face whenever he mentioned their heritage. "You're the only Cherokee I know."

"I can't help you, Adam. I don't follow the old ways anymore."

He scooted his chair forward. "Why not?" he pressed, hoping to uncover her mystery, unveil the true woman, the soul behind the quiet, exotic beauty.

She didn't respond. Instead she reached for her tea and held the mug, drawing comfort, it seemed, from the warmth.

He saw sadness in her eyes, the loneliness reflected in his own. They were meant to be part of each other's lives, he thought. He wouldn't let this lost angel fly away.

"I don't think being Cherokee is anything to be proud of," she said finally.

He didn't know how to react, so he waited for her to continue. She did, after she tasted her tea.

"When I was young my mother filled my head with all of those romantic notions about the old ways. I was taught to believe in the unity of family and have pride in my heritage." She met Adam's gaze, her voice distant. "Cherokee men were supposed to be warriors—their role to remain strong and provide for their wife and children."

"So who let you down, Sarah? Was it your father?"

She nodded. "When I was fourteen my mom died unexpectantly from an aneurysm. It was awful. I missed her so much. And so did my dad, but he buried himself in his grief. He didn't consider how I felt or how much I needed him. He just kept saying that he didn't want to go on without her."

For a moment Adam thought about his own parents, about the fact that they had died together. "I know how it feels to lose a parent. I lost both of mine, but maybe it's even harder losing a spouse, the person you planned to spend the rest of your life with."

Sarah gave him a hard stare. "Please don't make excuses for my father."

"I wasn't. I'm just trying to understand."

"What's to understand? My dad started drinking. He turned to alcohol for solace and let me fend for myself most of the time because he was too drunk to take responsibility."

Stunned, Adam only stared. This wasn't what he'd expected. All this time he had been wondering what plagued Sarah. And now he knew. It was her father's battle with alcoholism, a struggle Adam remembered well.

Frowning, he pictured himself before the addiction had set in—a lean, somewhat shy youth influenced and impressed by the "in" crowd. Parties, drinking games and teenage sex. He'd been tempted. And he'd fallen hard.

Should he tell Sarah? Admit that he'd drunk his way through high school?

Adam blew a heavy breath. Yes, he should tell her. But not now, not while she was finally opening up, revealing her troubled heart.

Besides, he wanted Sarah to think of him as someone she could lean on, and blurting out that he used to drink didn't seem to be the answer. Eventually he would talk about himself, explain that he wasn't like her father anymore. Adam had been clean for eleven years.

"Didn't anyone intervene?" he asked. "Try to get your dad some help?"

"Yes, but you can't force someone into sobriety."

Adam knew she was right. His parents had instilled "tough love," more or less forcing him into rehab, but he'd stayed sober on his own. "So your dad wasn't willing to quit?"

"He tried, I suppose, only not hard enough. Steadily he got worse. We were never rich, but his job as a mechanic provided a middle-class lifestyle. Eventually his drinking destroyed that, too. He started tipping the bottle at work and lost his job. I learned soon enough what it was like to be a poor downtrodden Indian." Her breath hitched, as unsteady and edgy as her words. "He never did regain regular employment, but he continued to offer promises of sobriety. And for the longest time I believed him."

"But you lost faith." Adam recalled how worried his parents had been. There was always the fear that he would slip up.

"I was tired of false promises. I left when I was eighteen, came to California to start over. It's the best thing I've ever done."

He wasn't inclined to think so, but he kept that thought to himself. Starting over didn't work if you left your heart behind. And Sarah's was still in Oklahoma, wishing her dad had come through.

"So you haven't seen your father or spoken to him in over six years?"

"That's right." She formed a steeple with her hands, much in the same manner Adam had been taught to pray. "Whenever my dad attempted to stop drinking and failed, he blamed his alcoholism on genetics. Indians can't help it, you see. It's in their blood. That certainly gave me a new perspective on being Cherokee." She tightened the steeple, lifted it to her chin. "Everything my mother told me was just illusion. Warriors don't exist anymore. Holding onto the old ways is pointless."

Sarah was making excuses, Adam thought sadly. She'd turned away from her heritage as a means to distance herself from a painful childhood. Rather than view her father as a man, she saw him as a fallen warrior—something intolerable in her mind.

Adam gazed up at the sky, at the stars shimmering in the heavens. Warriors were only human, men prone to fault—a fact Sarah needed to accept. Being Cherokee wasn't the cause of her father's demise and ignoring her culture wouldn't erase the despair he had caused.

A star winked from above, and Adam made a solemn vow. Somehow he was going to help this lost angel find her way home. And in the meantime, he'd keep his past a secret. Sarah might overreact to an addiction that had afflicted him years ago.

Four

————

Adam arrived at Sarah's apartment on Sunday afternoon. He had called ahead, so she was expecting him, but he still felt a little apprehensive. He didn't want to come on too strong, didn't want Sarah to know how easily she stirred his hormones. Adam was doing his damnedest to stick by their friendship agreement.

She opened the door and invited him in. "What did you bring?" she asked, eyeing the box he carried.

"Just some things I wanted to show you," he responded, hoping this was the right thing to do.

He placed the box on the floor and lifted the African violet he had tucked in the corner. First order of business, he thought, handing her the small potted plant. "This is for you."

"Thank you. It's lovely."

"My landlady grows them." And its exotic beauty reminded him of her, but he didn't say so.

He met her gaze, and she clutched the plant to her breast.

This sweltering summer day she wore a white T-shirt and denim shorts. She had shapely legs, a deep shade of copper, just the way he imagined the rest of her. And her feet were bare, her toenails painted a soft shade of pink. Barefoot women enticed Adam, the sexy, natural quality it seemed to give them.

She broke eye contact first, the flower still pressed against her body. "Make yourself at home, and I'll put this on the windowsill."

She headed for the kitchen, choosing just the right spot for the violet. He could see her from where he stood. Her hair was straight and dark, as thick as a midnight sky, swaying as she moved.

Because the image made him want her, he shifted his attention to her apartment. It was modern, with almond-colored carpeting and high ceilings. She had furnished it with a beige sofa and a glass-topped coffee table. The paintings on the walls displayed muted watercolors—a foaming seascape at dusk, a vase of willowy flowers, a white gazebo—serene, pretty things women enjoyed.

He noticed a small basket of seashells on the coffee table and smiled. He knew they were her way of connecting with nature, of breathing in the ocean and letting it flow through her veins. Like a wave. Warm and slow and mesmerizing.

Suddenly his body went taut, hungry with liquid heat. His belly tightened in a blatantly sexual pull, pressing lower, dangerously low. He had to stop wanting her, craving what he had vowed to avoid.

She returned from the kitchen, and he wished he was the sort of man who could go to another woman for relief, fall into bed with the first warm, willing body who came his way.

But even so, he knew that wouldn't work. It was Sarah he wanted, Sarah he longed to touch.

"I'm sorry," she said. "I'm being a terrible hostess. I didn't even offer you a cold drink."

"I'm fine. I don't need anything." Nothing but to get her out of his system, which he didn't see happening anytime soon. Here he was, at her home, intending to ask her to take a vacation with him—a woman he barely knew.

They settled onto the sofa, the box he'd brought on the table in front of them.

She peered into it curiously. "So what did you want to show me, Adam?"

"It's more or less my research material, literature I downloaded from web sites or photocopied from books."

"About adoption?"

He shook his head. "It's mostly Cherokee stuff." When she frowned, he continued, keeping his voice light. "There's also some information about Tahlequah. I called the Chamber of Commerce, and this is what they sent me." He lifted a large white packet bearing a black-and-white feather logo. It contained pamphlets about lodging, restaurants and schools, a couple of maps, pictures of recreational spots.

She didn't make a move for the packet, so he opened the flap, removed a brochure. "I'm going to Tahlequah in August, Sarah." Pausing a beat, he searched her gaze, smiled a little. "And I want you to go with me."

A stunned expression replaced the disapproving frown. "I can't do that."

"Why not?"

"Because I..." She released an audible breath, her explanation drifting. "Are you planning to search for your mother?"

"Yes. I realize she might not live in Oklahoma anymore, but she could still have family there. And I was born in Tahlequah. I want to see what's it like, absorb whatever I can." He paged through the brochure. It contained information about the Cherokee Heritage Center. "You're familiar with the area, Sarah. You could be my guide."

"I don't think that's a good idea."

"I'll pay your way. And I'm not asking you to stay with me." He kept his gaze trained on hers and saw her eyelids flutter. She had captivating eyes, long pretty lashes. It was all he could do not to lose himself in them. "We'll get separate rooms."

"I wasn't worried about..."

Her copper skin flushed, and he realized how shy Sarah was, how innocently sensual. That, God forbid, made him want her again.

He looked away, gained his composure. This trip wasn't a whim. He hadn't conjured it as a ruse to be near her. He honestly believed it could present a new beginning for both of them. He could search for his mother, and Sarah could get reacquainted with her roots. She needed to see her dad one more time—ask for an apology, insist he get help.

Rather than push the issue, he gave her a measure of space, time to adjust to the idea of going back to the place she had left behind. "You don't have to make a decision right now. Just promise you'll think about it."

"I won't change my mind, Adam."

He shrugged, sent her a friendly smile. "You might. And if you don't, then I'll make the trip alone."

"You should let it go," she said. "Pretend you never stumbled upon those adoption papers."

"I can't do that." He would search until his dying day, search until he met the people who had created him, looked in their eyes and saw a piece of himself. Did he have his mother's cheekbones? His father's hands? "I know you don't understand. But my adoptive parents are gone, and now I'm alone. I need answers."

"What if you don't like what you find?"

"Then I'll deal with it. Life is full of challenges. And mankind has flaws. None of us are perfect."

"You are," she said, stunning him nearly speechless.

"Where did you get that idea?"

"You're tall and handsome and smart. It's hard to find fault."

"You need to look deeper, Sarah. I'm no different than anyone else."

"But you are," she countered. "You're not only handsome, but you have a good heart."

Adam felt a rush of guilt. A good heart, maybe, but not an honest one. He still hadn't told her about his unholy past.

"Sarah, I—"

What was he going to say? He used to pimp beer? Steal whiskey? Belt back a shot or two before school?

Suddenly he couldn't bear to admit the truth. Because deep down, he knew it would destroy the clean, tender emotion stirring between them.

"I'm just an average guy," he managed, telling himself it wasn't a complete lie. For the past eleven years, he'd lived a pretty normal life.

"Not to me. I've never known anyone like you."

Immediately they both fell silent, the kind of quiet that marked an awkward moment. She chewed her bottom lip, and he studied the archway that led to her spotless kitchen. Slats of gold streamed through the blinds, shooting filtered sunlight into the room.

He wanted to touch her, slide his hands down her arms, feel the pulse at her wrist. But instead he lifted the Tahlequah packet and removed the entire contents. The papers made a ruffling noise, and Sarah turned toward the sound.

The brochure on top caught Sarah's eye, and she noticed a heading that read "Self-guided tour of historic Tahlequah." Adam wanted her to serve as his guide, return to Oklahoma for two weeks.

Home. He wanted her to go home.

A burst of panic constricted her throat. She couldn't go back. Wouldn't go back, especially with him. He confused her emotions, reminding her of starry Oklahoma nights and the Cherokee warriors her mother used to talk about.

Caught up in the image of a warrior, she studied him. His hair was combed away from his face, secured at his nape in a thick ponytail. She had never seen him with his hair down and couldn't help but wonder how it would look flowing over his shoulders.

Adam shifted the papers on his lap, reached for a map and unfolded it. "Where did you live?" he asked.

Sarah forced herself to look at the map, to quell the anxiety in the pit of her stomach. She leaned into him. She could smell the faint aroma of the soap he used. She had seen a bar of it in his bathroom, knew it contained extracts of pine and European mosses.

"In this area," she said, picturing the friendly middle-class neighborhood: Sunday-afternoon barbecues filling the summer air, children's bicycles parked hastily on freshly mowed lawns, teenage boys tinkering with hand-me-down cars. "They used to come to our door and ask for his opinion."

Adam glanced up from the map. "What? Who?"

Sarah blinked, realizing she had spoken her thoughts out loud. "Some of the teenage boys in our neighborhood. My dad would help them customize their cars, make them louder or faster or whatever it was they were trying to accomplish." She shivered at the memory. Happy times, before her mother had died, before her father had crawled into his vodka-steeped hole.

"Your dad must have been a good mechanic."

She shrugged. "He was, I suppose." But *was* was the operative word. Like everything else, he had let his career fall by the wayside. After his wife had died, nothing mattered to William Cloud.

"I really want to go here," Adam said.

She glanced at the map again, saw that he referred to the Cherokee Heritage Center.

"Have you been there?" he asked.

She nodded, knowing she couldn't avoid Adam's questions. He had such raw need on his face, a thirst to hear about anything that would put him in touch with his ancestry. She sincerely hoped his quest wouldn't end up hurting him, but she had her doubts. Not just because of the Indian aspect, but because most adopted people who searched for their biological families ended up with ill-fated reunions, strangers with nothing in common but the blood that ran through their veins.

"My mom used to take me to the Heritage Center," she said finally. "It was one of her favorite places. The prayer chapel affected her the most. It's dedicated to the Cherokees who lost their lives on the Trail of Tears." And now the chapel reminded Sarah of her mother, a woman who died believing in dreams.

"You must miss her terribly," he said, as though reading her mind.

"I do, but I've learned to go on."

"Do you miss your dad at all?"

She lifted one shoulder, lowered it in a partial shrug. "I miss the way he once was, I suppose. But now I realize that wasn't really him. He tried to be what my mother wanted him to be. She was the traditional Cherokee, the one who spoke the language and followed the old ways."

Adam sat quietly for a moment, then said, "I appreciate your talking to me about this. I know it's not easy for you. But it's been tough on me, too. I feel like I'm on the outside looking in. I don't even know if I'm supposed to say *Native American* or *Indian*." He picked up the brochures, slipped them back into the oversize envelope. "I don't want to do or say the wrong thing."

He was trying so hard to find his place in the world, she thought. This perfect, beautiful man. "Use whatever term you're comfortable with."

"I notice you say *Indian*."

"That's what I'm used to."

"It's a little confusing," he said.

She had to smile. "Don't worry about trying to be so politically correct, and you'll get along just fine. You could never offend anyone, Adam."

He smiled back at her, and her stomach fluttered. That gorgeous, white smile. No, he could never offend, only charm.

"I guess you're what's considered an urban Indian," she said, explaining when he gave her a curious look. "Someone who wasn't raised on a reservation or in a traditional environment."

"Yeah, but I'm sure the other urbanites know more about their culture than I do."

"Not necessarily. There are plenty of elders who didn't pass on the old ways. They grew up with the stigma of being Indian, and some of them thought it would be easier to spare future generations the same fate. So as the years went by, holding onto the culture became less important.''

"But times have changed. I read that they're even teaching some of the native languages in colleges now.''

"Things haven't changed that much.'' At least not for Sarah. The stigma was still there, deep in her bones.

He reached for her hand, touched it. "I wish I could make it better for you.''

Sarah shivered, but she wasn't cold. A heat, an incredible warmth, flowed through her. His touch, his hand on hers—that simple gesture made her want him.

He could make it better, she thought, if he would kiss her again. Unable to stop herself, she leaned into him.

He moved closer, too. Only he moved slowly, cautiously, questioning her gaze, asking for permission with his eyes.

"Yes,'' she whispered, an instant before his lips brushed hers.

He was gentle, reverent. He slid his hands to her waist, held lightly. She didn't want to close her eyes, didn't want to lose sight of him, but a dreamy sensation washed over her and she yielded to it, her eyelids fluttering.

No longer could she see him, but she could feel him—every movement, every tingle, every erotic tremble he incited. The skin over his cheekbones was taut, his jaw freshly shaven. She lifted her hand and skimmed his hair, the smooth, silky texture that led to that carefully secured ponytail.

As she cupped the back of his neck, he sucked her bottom lip, sucked until she moaned and fisted his shirt, pulling him even closer.

They knocked over the box he'd brought, spilling envelopes and papers onto the carpet. Neither paid attention to it. Instead they went a little crazy, their mouths meeting over and over, tongues diving and dancing.

The room spun like a carousel, but she didn't care if she was confused and dizzy. All that mattered was him. This man. This incredible, perfect man.

"Adam,'' she said his name out loud, breathed it through another spiraling kiss.

With both hands still grasping his shirt, her mind wandered into sexual delirium. What would it be like to unbutton all that rough denim? Place her hand on his chest? Let his heartbeat thud against her palm?

Would his skin feel as golden, as warm as it seemed radiating through his clothes? Her mind continued to spin, and he lifted her onto his lap, so that she straddled him.

As the buttons on his fly grazed her zipper, moisture, hot and honeyed, settled between her legs. From the friction she thought. They were rubbing against each other, denim pressing denim—his jeans, her shorts. He skimmed her bare leg, and Sarah's nipples went hard and achy. She wanted him to touch her there, too. Caress her with those fire-tipped fingers.

Suddenly a noise jarred her—a loud, persistent ringing.

Sarah thought it was a warning bell screaming in her head, but when Adam pulled back, she realized he had heard it, too.

Struggling to gain her composure, she blinked through blurred vision. She was still dizzy, still drugged with feminine arousal. Adam seemed dazed, too. His eyelids looked heavy, and his breathing sounded raspy, as though he couldn't quite steady it.

"Was that the phone?" he asked.

She glanced around her apartment, hardly recognizing it. Why wouldn't her eyes focus, her heart quit pounding? "I don't know." Where was the phone? she wondered.

The sound buzzed again, and recognition shot through her. "It's the doorbell. Someone's at the door."

Instantly the room came into view. The afternoon sun blared through the blinds, and Sarah squinted at the box they had knocked onto the floor.

Remembering the brochures from Tahlequah, she stood. Adam wanted to take her to Oklahoma, bring her back into the world she had left behind.

What in God's name had she been thinking, encouraging him to kiss her? Run his hands over her body?

Adam rose from the sofa, a portion of his shirt untucked and slightly rumpled from where she had tugged on it. Sarah pulled air into her lungs, knowing he was aroused beneath the button-fly jeans.

He was so incredibly gorgeous. A tall, dangerous temptation.

"I have to get the door," she said.

"Then I'll clean up."

He knelt to right the cardboard box, his voice lower and huskier than she would have liked.

Crossing the room, she avoided his gaze. She wouldn't allow herself to look at him again, get drawn into those hypnotic eyes or that warm, wet mouth. His sex-tinged voice was torture enough. She could still taste him, and her nipples remained hard, her flesh tingling.

She paused at the door, took a calming breath. Maybe a zealous youth selling magazine subscriptions waited on the other side, someone friendly and safe she could invite into the apartment, use as a shield between herself and Adam.

Placing her hand on the knob, she opened the door.

"Oh, thank goodness you're home."

Vicki Lester sighed from apparent relief. She was Sarah's neighbor, an easy-going woman who looked uncharacteristically frazzled. Her curly red hair was pinned haphazardly to her head, ringlets springing against her freckled face.

Sarah stepped back, inviting Vicki inside. "Are you all right?"

"No. Yes. I mean, I'm fine, but my baby-sitter just called in sick."

"Where are the girls?"

"At a friend's house, but I have to pick them up soon." Vicki turned, apparently catching sight of the man in Sarah's apartment. "Adam," she said, her voice less jittery. "I didn't realize you were here."

Adam and Vicki knew each other, of course. She was the one who had told him about Sarah in the first place. And she had questioned Sarah about him later, asking her what she'd thought of him.

Adam stepped forward, and Sarah noticed his shirt had been neatly tucked into his pants, even if the pre-washed denims still rode low and sexy on his hips. Keeping her gaze above his belt buckle, she averted them from the button fly. She didn't want to be reminded that she had been straddling his lap, rubbing herself against him like one of his cats.

She didn't want Vicki to figure it out, either. The other woman, she suspected, had wanted them to get together from the beginning. She doubted it had been a deliberate match-maker attempt, but a hopeful one just the same.

Adam stood beside Sarah. "I just stopped by for a visit," he said to the redhead. "So what's this about your baby-sitter?"

Vicki pushed a rebellious curl away from her face. "She's sick and can't watch my daughters. And here I am scheduled for a seminar in Arizona tomorrow. I'm flying out tonight, or I will be if I can find someone to stay with the girls." She blew a tired-sounding breath. "And I just got a promotion, too. My boss will be fit to be tied if I miss this seminar."

Sarah sympathized with Vicki's plight. The thirty-five-year-old divorcée worked hard to provide for her daughters, especially since her ex-husband was a deadbeat dad who shirked his financial responsibilities. And if there was one thing Sarah detested, it was men who neglected their children.

"I can stay with the girls," she offered before Vicki had to ask. "I have Sundays and Mondays off."

The redhead gave her a sturdy hug. "You're a lifesaver. I swear I'll pay you back somehow."

"I'd be glad to help out, too," Adam said. "If you don't mind having a big guy like me sleeping on your couch."

"Are you kidding?" Vicki grabbed him for a hug. "The more responsible adults the better. I hate leaving the girls overnight as it is." She stepped back and grinned. "And I'm sure my couch will survive."

But what about me? Sarah thought. How will I survive being in the same house with Adam all night? She glanced back at the sofa, the spot where she and Adam had practically mauled each other.

They would be baby-sitting, she reminded herself. She wouldn't be spending the night with him all by herself. Two bright-eyed little girls would be there. How dangerous could that be?

"What time should we come by?" she asked Vicki. Baby-sitting aside, the *we* part sounded oddly intimate, as though she and Adam were a couple.

"About 5:00 p.m. I already have a casserole in the fridge for dinner, so all you have to do is bake it." She adjusted her handbag. "The girls are supposed to be in bed by 8:30, but I can't guarantee they'll go willingly."

"Don't worry," Sarah assured her. "Everything will be fine."

Vicki departed, offering her thanks again. Once Sarah and Adam were alone, she became overly aware of his masculine presence, the size of his hands, the muscles in his arms, the way they flexed when he moved.

"Have you met Vicki's children?" she asked, before silence threatened to swallow them whole.

He shook his head. "No, but she's told me a lot about them."

Sarah shifted her bare feet. Silence again, the only sound the hum of the central air conditioner. She couldn't think of anything else to say, and she didn't know quite where to look.

Adam checked his watch. "I should get going. I'll meet you at Vicki's apartment at five, okay?"

"Okay."

He headed toward the couch, picked up the box containing his Cherokee research. "Bye, sweet Sarah. I'll see you later."

The nickname hit her square in the chest, jump-starting her heart. Every time he said it, she felt young and innocent.

She met his gaze. "Bye, Adam." Closing the door after him, she leaned against it and slowly, very slowly, caught her breath.

Five

By 5:30 p.m. Vicki was on her way to the airport, and Sarah and Adam were alone with two little girls. Sarah set the dining-room table and watched the kitchen activity with interest.

Mandy, the eight-year-old, hadn't said more than a few quiet words. She stood at the counter while dinner was being prepared, filling a restaurant-style napkin dispenser. She was a serene child, with strawberry-blond hair and fair skin.

Dawn, the six-year-old, had the same light complexion, only her nose was dusted with freckles and her hair, as red as a fire engine, grew from her head like a curly mop.

She had volunteered to help Adam fix a salad, so she wiggled beside him, eager to work. Tearing the lettuce with gusto, she grinned up at him, displaying a wide, friendly gap between two slightly crooked front teeth. Her vibrant personality was as animated as her Raggedy-Ann looks.

Although she had been bombarding him with questions, he didn't seem to mind. He answered her patiently, all the while giving her something to do. Sarah learned that red was

Adam's favorite color and that he liked to count the stars at night and watch the news in the morning. He chatted with Dawn, but still seemed completely aware of Mandy, the timid eight-year-old who kept stealing glances at him when she thought he wasn't looking.

Mandy, Sarah realized, had developed an instant crush on Adam. The fact that she was a child hadn't immunized her to his charm.

Adam opened the refrigerator, then turned and caught Sarah's eye from across the room. He smiled, and the persistent winged flutter started up in her stomach. At that he's-so-gorgeous moment, she knew exactly how little Mandy felt.

They shared dinner twenty minutes later, gathered around a glass-topped table. Vicki's apartment was similar to Sarah's, only homier. She supposed it was the youthful touches, the adolescent artwork attached to the refrigerator door and the colored pencils and toys the girls left in the living room. The apartment seemed lived in, the attractive furnishings exhibiting signs of wear. Sarah's environment seemed lonely by comparison.

Mandy continued to study Adam through her lashes, although she remained quiet, eating the tamale pie her mother had prepared earlier. When Adam winked at the child, Sarah's heart warmed. He knew—sensitive, kind, gorgeous Adam knew—the little girl wanted him to notice her.

"Is your real name Amanda?" he asked.

She nodded.

He buttered a slice of bread, set it on his plate. "Do you know what Amanda means?"

She shook her head.

"It has a Latin origin," he told her. "And it means 'much loved.'"

"How do you know that?" she asked, watching every move he made.

"I had a girlfriend named Amanda. She was pretty and blond, like you."

That bit of personal news appeared to please the child. She

accepted the compliment in a shy, ladylike fashion, dropping her gaze and smiling into her plate.

Sarah, on the other hand, found herself wondering about Adam's Amanda. Pretty and blond conjured a tall, blue-eyed California-girl image—so unlike herself. And although his former girlfriend shouldn't concern her, she couldn't stop the sudden snap of unwarranted jealousy.

"What does my name mean?" Dawn asked, air whistling through her front teeth.

Adam tilted his head and studied the younger girl. "Hmm. I'll bet it has something to do with the start of a new day." He lifted his fork, sent her a smile. "Have you ever watched the sunrise at dawn? It's mighty pretty."

Dawn grinned, glanced at Sarah, then back at Adam. "Do you know what Sarah's name means?"

He turned and met her gaze. She wanted to look away, but couldn't. His eyes, those warm brown eyes, had her sinking into their depths.

"Princess," he said quietly. "It means princess."

Sarah knew the origin of her name, but on Adam's lips it sounded gentle, sensual, like part of a fairy tale. The princess and the dragon slayer. What would happen if she let herself fall into that fantasy?

She would get swept away, she thought, pulled into a world that held no realm of reality. Lifting her water, she broke eye contact. She, of all people, knew fairy tales didn't exist.

"The name Adam is from the Bible," Dawn said, clearly fascinated with the subject.

"Yes, it is," he responded. "That's why my parents picked it for me."

The chatty little girl scratched her freckled nose, smearing tamale sauce across her face. "And Sarah's parents must have called her Sarah 'cause they thought she was a princess."

Adam's voice turned husky, just enough for Sarah to feel the masculine sound slipping through her bones.

"I have no doubt that's the reason," he said. "No doubt at all."

She gazed at the dragon slayer named Adam, the man who

dreamed of finding his parents, of reuniting old lovers. Maybe fairy tales should be allowed, at least for tonight. After all, they were spending the evening with two bright-eyed little girls.

The two bright-eyed little girls didn't want to go to bed, even after hours of their favorite board game. But a second helping of ice cream finally convinced them to bathe and put their pajamas on.

They shared a frilly pink room that reminded Sarah of being a child herself—sugar and spice and everything nice. That was, she thought, a long time ago.

Mandy and Dawn were each in their own bed, the covers tucked around them. Dawn kept a worn-out doll with her, and Mandy watched Adam with stars in her eyes. Somehow he had managed to give the smitten eight-year-old special attention without neglecting her younger sister.

Adam sat on the edge of Mandy's bed and looked up at Sarah. "Why don't you tell the girls about the Cherokee Little People. I would do it, but all I know is what I've read. You're probably more familiar with them."

She blinked, then stepped forward. Adam had just tapped into her childhood. Her mother used to talk about the Little People, telling Sarah about them. Of course, it wasn't common practice to discuss them after nightfall. But apparently Adam wasn't aware of that.

She took a seat on Dawn's bed, and the child gazed at her with expectation. Mandy and Adam watched her, too, waiting, it seemed, to be drawn into the world of Cherokee superstition.

She decided she could talk about the Little People at night. Particularly since the old ways were no longer a part of her life.

"They're called *Ynwi Tsunndi*," she said. "And they live in rock caves on mountainsides." With a wave of unexpected emotion, she paused, suddenly uncomfortable about breaking tradition. "Most Cherokees don't talk about them after the sun goes down. I'll tell you what I know, but after tonight, you can't mention them in the evening ever again.''

Dawn and Mandy made that solemn vow, and Adam sent Sarah an apologetic look, realizing he had erred. She dismissed his blunder with a gentle glance. If the Little People truly existed, they would forgive a man like Adam.

''Are they smaller than me?'' Dawn asked.

Sarah nodded. ''They barely reach a man's knee. But they're handsome, and their hair falls almost to the ground.''

The anxious child interrupted again. ''Are they nice?''

''Very nice,'' Sarah said, smiling at Adam when his expression softened. ''They're helpful and kindhearted, and they like kids. If a child gets lost in the mountains, the Little People will take them back to their parents.'' She brushed a lock of hair off her shoulder. ''They help sad boys and girls, too.''

Clearly enthralled with this information, the six-year-old pushed her blanket away. ''Are they like leprechauns?''

''Sort of. Sometimes they can be mischievous, but they don't chase pots of gold. The Little People spend most of their time drumming and dancing. But you're not allowed to search for their home. If you do, they'll cast a spell on you and make you dazed for the rest of your life.''

Dawn shook her head vigorously, sending red curls dancing around her face. ''I won't try to find their house.''

''They don't have a house,'' her sister said, as though trying to sound more grown-up than her eight years. ''They're not real. It's just a story.''

''They do too have a house,'' the younger one insisted. ''They live in a cave in the mountains. The Little People are real, aren't they, Sarah?''

She caught Adam watching her, the man searching for his roots. ''There are a lot of Cherokee people who think so,'' she said. ''And you can never be sure if they're around, because if they don't want you to see them, they become invisible.''

''See.'' Dawn made a face at her older sibling.

Mandy frowned, then turned to Adam ''Do you think they're real?''

He patted the child's ankle through the blanket. "I think the world is full of magic, especially in the forests and mountains. So I would just as soon not disturb the Little Peoples' home. I wouldn't want to be dazed for the rest of my life."

When Mandy agreed that the Little People might actually exist, he leaned toward her and asked for a hug good-night, telling the girls it was time for sleep.

She hugged him, and when her head hit the pillow, Sarah thought she looked a bit glassy-eyed. Adam's charm had dazed the eight-year-old far more than a spell from the Little People ever could.

He hugged Dawn as well, and Sarah followed suit, embracing both children. She turned off the light, and Adam led her out of the room.

He had brought a box of herbal tea along, so they brewed a pot and sat on Vicki's floral-printed sofa, sipping the mint-flavored drink.

He stretched his legs, looking devastatingly male, a bright blue T-shirt tucked into the waistband of stylish jeans. Sarah found herself wondering if they buttoned or zipped, then turned away, embarrassed by the provocative thought.

"I'm sorry," he said. "I didn't know that you weren't supposed to talk about them at night."

Sarah turned back. Because he was glancing around as though invisible beings might be watching him, she smiled. Her mother would have adored him.

"It's okay. Like you said, you didn't know." She sipped her tea, savoring the mint. "But traditional Cherokees don't describe them as being magical or supernatural. Spiritual beings are a part of their everyday world."

"Really?" His expression turned thoughtful. "To me, it all seems like magic. Everything about the Cherokee is so beautiful, so wondrous."

Oh, yes, she decided. Her mother would have adored this man.

They both fell silent, companionable quiet between them. Tonight she couldn't fault him for wanting to know about his heritage.

He placed his cup on the coffee table and rolled his shoulders. The movement rippled his T-shirt. Sarah couldn't help herself. Her roving eyes strayed to his jeans again. "Do you plan on having kids someday?" he asked.

She chewed her bottom lip. The question didn't seem out of place, not when they had just tucked two little girls into bed. "I'm not sure. I adore children, but marriage has never really been a conscious thought." At least not until now, she realized, wondering what sort of husband Adam would make. Sarah had abandoned her girlish dreams long ago, but Adam was renewing a part of her that ached for the past. The happy times, the years she believed in love.

How had she gotten so cynical? So grown-up and jaded?

Adam shifted in his seat, drawing her attention back to him. "I want as many children as my wife is willing to give me," he said. "And that's one of the reasons I'm determined to find my biological parents. They're part of who I am, a legacy I can pass on to my kids."

"What about your adoptive family? That doesn't seem fair to them. They're the ones who raised you."

"Having a relationship with my biological parents won't diminish the memory of my adoptive parents. I intend to tell my children about them. I have photo albums filled with pictures." His voice turned quiet. "It hurts that they didn't tell me the truth about the adoption, but I still love them."

As a wave of sudden sadness drifted through the room, Sarah brushed his hand, offering comfort. He glanced out the window at the darkness outside, and her heart went out to him—this tall, handsome man who was all alone in the world. Sarah was alone, too, but she had made the choice consciously.

His childhood had been so normal, she thought. So different from hers. And Adam's parents had never meant to hurt him. They had wanted him for their son. To Sarah, adopting someone else's child was a loving, caring act.

"Have you ever been in a relationship serious enough to consider marriage?" she asked.

"No. I've been in a couple of fairly serious relationships

before, but I've haven't met anyone I considered spending the rest of my life with.'' He smiled a little. ''I've never been in love, but I'm sure I'll know when it happens. I'll know who the right woman is.'' He paused, trapped her gaze. ''What about you, sweet Sarah? Ever lost your heart?''

''No.'' She shook her head, fearful she could be losing it now. Everything about Adam seemed so right.

A Cherokee knight. A dragon slayer.

Breaking eye contact, she rose. She was falling into the fairy tale she had created, and she had to stop herself from tumbling too far. ''I should get ready for bed. The girls will probably be up early.'' And she couldn't spend the rest of the evening imagining what kind of husband Adam would make. ''I'll bring you a sheet and a blanket for the couch.''

''I need a pillow, too.''

She went down the hall, and when she returned with the bedding, she noticed he had cleared their tea cups from the coffee table. He stood beside the sofa, in his stylish T-shirt and jeans. His thumbs were hooked in his pockets—a stance that made the female in her take notice.

She placed the bundle on the couch.

''Thanks.'' He smiled at her, something he did far too often. ''I'm going to shower, then watch TV for a while. I'll keep it low so it doesn't bother you.''

''I'm a heavy sleeper,'' she said, disturbed by the image her mind had conjured. Adam taking a shower in one bathroom while she bathed in another. They would be naked at the same time, in the house. A flush of heat crept up her neck.

She lifted her hand, felt the fire spread. The image wouldn't go away. In her mind's eye she saw him—his athletic body glistening with water, that long brown hair loose and wet.

It was time to end this, cool her skin, bid him a proper, if not impersonal, good-night. But just as she prepared her escape, he said her name in a voice as smooth and rich as cream.

''Sarah. Sweet Sarah.''

She didn't move, not a single muscle. Her feet froze to the floor.

He took a step toward her. "We still haven't talked about what happened earlier."

For a moment, she feared she would do something humiliating, like faint. She couldn't seem to catch her breath, get enough oxygen to her brain. He expected her to talk about the way they had kissed that afternoon, rubbed and caressed through their clothes?

"We're just friends." The statement sounded foolish, even to her own ears.

He glanced up at the ceiling as though collecting his thoughts. When he brought his gaze back to hers, his eyes were intense, hypnotic. "I keep telling myself that very same thing. We're just friends. There's nothing happening between us." He laughed a little, a rough, textured sound that faded as quickly as it came on. "That's a lie, at least for me. I can't help myself. I want you. And I can't pretend that I don't." He moved closer, enough to put them inches apart. "I even fantasize about you wearing that red dress, the one with the dragon on it. Only you're naked under it. Naked just for me." He touched her cheek, then drew back. "You're my midnight seduction, sweet Sarah."

Her heart thumped wildly. She wanted to kiss him, seduce him, feel the dragon branding her skin. Mist and moonlight, she thought. Fairy tales and fantasies. God help her. She craved all of that and more.

Nerves tangled in her stomach, coiled then twisted into chains. Should she tell him that she was a virgin? That her experiences were limited? Would it shock him? Make him view her differently?

"I want you, too," was all she could manage to say before she turned and walked away, her lungs fighting for air.

When she reached the master bedroom, she sat on the edge of the bed, her legs wobbly. She had left the door open, and a short time later, she heard water running down the hall. Adam was taking a shower.

Sarah stood and closed the door, imagining what it would feel like to slip into the tiny stall with him, slide her hands all over that strong, muscular body. Live out her erotic fantasy.

She began to remove her clothes, but as she picked up her robe, she headed for the bathroom just a few feet away.

Wanting Adam didn't mean she had the courage to take him.

Adam squinted into the morning light. It blasted through the window, drenching him in its blinding glow. He had left the drapes open last night. Mostly because he hadn't slept well and the moon and stars had seemed like good company.

He didn't need to analyze his restless night. He knew the cause. Sarah—sweet, sweet Sarah. Her erotic admission still played in his mind.

I want you, too.

Last night had been torture. His mouth had all but watered, hungry for the taste of a dark-eyed, dark-haired woman. His midnight fantasy. His lust-driven seduction.

Rubbing his eyes, he rose and began to fold the sheet. The blanket came next, and when they were both stacked neatly on the sofa, he headed for the bathroom, an overnight bag in hand. Sarah and the girls were still asleep, but he assumed they would awaken soon, which meant he should brush his teeth, wash his face and comb his tousled hair. He looked like a man who had been up most of the night. Shaving would help, too, he supposed. He pulled his hand across his chin, felt the roughness. His beard stubble wasn't heavy, but it was still there, peppering his jaw.

Adam went through his grooming routine, aware of every move, his muscles rolling and bunching. He still felt a tingle of eroticism, and he was doing his damnedest to shake it. There were children in the house, and that made him guilty as hell. How did parents do it? he wondered. How did they lust after each other when their kids were stumbling out of bed, pajamas rumpled, security blankets and stuffed animals trailing behind them?

Adam left the bathroom, his hair slicked back and banded into its usual ponytail, a cotton shirt tucked into a pair of loose, comfortable khakis. Maybe some cartoons would knock the heat out of him. He would turn on the TV and wait for the kids.

He didn't wait long. They came into the living room just as he had pictured them, rumpled and sleepy-eyed. Curls sprang from Dawn's head, like the spiral noodles his mother used to smother in red sauce. On the child's feet were slippers that sported tiny pink pompoms.

Spotting him, she grinned and wiggled her nose, sending freckles dancing across a pixie face.

"Hey, pumpkin," he said. "How are you?"

"Good, but there's something important I have to say." She moved closer, taking each step with caution. "It's daytime now, so it's okay to talk about the Little People, right?"

He nodded, grateful the child had taken Sarah's warning seriously. Adam wasn't one to dismiss ancient beliefs.

"The Little People sneaked into our room last night," Dawn announced quietly.

He couldn't help but smile. "Really?"

"Uh-huh." As she bobbed her head, noodles bounced in disarray. "But I didn't hear 'em 'cause I was asleep."

Adam looked past her, catching Mandy's gaze. The eight-year-old stood back, watching him through intense blue eyes. He was used to women getting spongy over him, but not young girls. It was, he decided, a responsibility he couldn't ignore. Innocent hearts broke much too easily.

"Did you hear the Little People?" he asked her, hoping she would say yes, treat her baby sister to a thrill. Dawn's heart was innocent, too.

"Of course not."

Adam withheld a frown. Mandy was shy and pretty and much too self-conscious. She needed to believe in magic and legends and spiritual beings. Last night he had convinced her that the Little People might exist, but apparently this morning she felt foolish about the whole thing.

"Just because you didn't hear them doesn't mean they weren't there," Dawn said, eager for her sister to verify her story.

Mandy spared the younger girl a tolerant glance, but when Dawn's eyes began to water, the tolerant look turned sisterly.

"I suppose they could have climbed up the balcony," she relinquished. "And the neighbors wouldn't have seen them if they were invisible."

Bouncing, Dawn said, "I knew it! I just knew they sneaked in."

Adam thanked Mandy with a pleased smile. She blushed something fierce, but returned his smile with one of her own.

He watched cartoons with the girls, feeling calm and fatherly. But the moment Sarah came into the room, his nervous system went haywire. His mouth was suddenly dry, his heart beat faster, his palms turned clammy, uncharacteristic reactions he couldn't seem to stop.

Her hair was freshly washed, long and damp and fragrant. He could actually smell her shampoo, or at least he thought he did. His imagination may have conjured the botanical perfume.

Dawn greeted Sarah enthusiastically, recounting the tale about the Little People sneaking into the house last night.

"Even Mandy says so," the younger girl proclaimed.

Sarah smiled, and Adam studied Mandy's reaction. The older girl didn't say much, but she watched Sarah through those young, serious eyes. It was obvious that the child admired the Cherokee woman, maybe even imagined herself growing up to be like her.

There were already similarities, he thought. Not in their appearance, but in the way they moved, talked, kept themselves distanced from others. They were both beautiful, both mysterious and challenging.

Sarah had yet to glance his way. Last night she'd claimed she wanted him, but this morning she avoided his gaze. Years from now, Mandy would probably do the same thing to some smitten young man. Adam already sympathized with the guy.

"What should we have for breakfast?" Sarah asked the girls.

"Pancakes," came the joint reply.

Sarah tossed that luxurious damp hair behind her and rolled

up her sleeves. She wore no makeup and plain clothes, but to Adam, she could have been a barefoot siren—a beguiling forest nymph with copper skin and exotic eyes.

She finally looked up and met his gaze. "Good morning," she said.

The simple greeting hit him square in the solar plexus. He nearly lost his next breath, then cursed himself for wanting her so badly.

"Do you need some help with breakfast?" he asked.

"Sure."

Her tone sounded casual, but he sensed a flutter of nervousness behind it. Good, he thought. He wasn't the only one suffering, feeling awkward and unsteady.

The girls remained in front of the TV, and Adam and Sarah headed for the kitchen. Their baby-sitting duties wouldn't end until this evening, so they still had hours and hours to go. Adam decided he'd better get used to the sensation humming between them, the erotic vibration that had become thick and much too tangible.

She rummaged through the cabinet, found a box of instant pancake mix, then began searching for something else.

"I can't reach it," she said, indicating a mixing bowl on a high shelf.

Adam moved in beside her and retrieved the bowl. It hadn't been his imagination. Her hair was gloriously fragrant, a blend of cloves and carnations. No wonder she teased his libido. Carnations were a known aphrodisiac—a sweet, spicy flower that increased sexual desire.

I'm doomed, he thought, wishing he could pull her into his arms, tangle his hands in her hair, kiss her until they both gasped for air.

"Will you dice some fruit?" she asked.

"Adam?" she asked when he didn't respond.

"Yeah?"

"Would you rather make the pancakes?"

He stepped back, away from her. "No. I'll dice the fruit." He didn't have the slightest idea how to make pancakes, and now wasn't the time to learn.

Wielding a paring knife, he set about his task. And although he told himself to ignore her, he kept stealing glances. Every so often she stole glances at him, too—those dark eyes catching his for an instant, as quick and jumpy as his heartbeat.

She mixed the pancake batter with a brisk motion, but when she stopped to taste it, to lift a dripping dollop to her mouth, a white-hot flame ignited in his belly.

I've got it bad, he thought, deliberately shifting his gaze to the cutting board.

He focused on the fruit, on the apples and bananas and summer peaches. He wasn't a teenager saddled with raging hormones. He was a twenty-nine-year-old, a grown man capable of controlling primal urges.

Satisfied he had won that battle, Adam peeled an orange, his hands deft and steady. Much more relaxed, he took a deep breath, let it out slowly. The mental reminder that he was pushing thirty seemed to do the trick.

The patter of little feet caught his attention. Dawn skipped into the kitchen, red curls bouncing to keep up. He glanced down at her slippers and smiled. The pompoms danced, too.

Little girls. Daughters. He wanted a house full.

"Are the pancakes ready?" the child asked.

"Just about, sweetie," Sarah said. "Why don't you and your sister set the table?"

Suddenly the morning turned noisy and chaotic, with silverware clanking and young voices chattering. Sarah flipped pancakes while Adam poured glasses of milk and served fresh fruit.

They ate in the dining room, cartoons flickering in the background. Adam looked across the cluttered table at Sarah. Her hair had begun to dry to a glossy black sheen, as soft and elusive as a raven's wing.

The feeling that rushed his system wasn't lust. It was something more akin to romance, to family. He wondered what it would be like to make a life with her, to brush her lips tenderly, to watch her tummy swell with his child.

Soon, Adam thought, as guilt consumed him, soon he would have to tell Sarah the truth about his past. He couldn't keep deceiving a woman whose father was an alcoholic.

A woman who had managed to become his obsession.

Six

Vicki returned a little after 9:00 p.m., looking like a travel-worn businesswoman in a navy-blue suit and silk blouse. Her curly red hair was coiled into a tidy French twist, but pale shadows dogged her eyes.

"How was the seminar?" Sarah asked.

Vicki plopped down on the couch and sighed. "Good. Long. I'm glad I was only scheduled for one day."

Sarah sat beside her. "The girls are asleep already."

The other woman slipped off her pumps. "I hope they didn't give you any trouble."

"They were perfect angels." This came from Adam, who stood in the living room a little awkwardly.

Sarah knew the feeling. Since the children had gone to bed, she and Adam didn't know what to do with themselves, where to focus their gazes, what to talk about.

Vicki looked up at Adam and smiled. "Thank you. That's just what a mother wants to hear."

"No problem. It's the truth." He shifted his stance, smiled

back at her. "Do you have any more luggage in the car? I'd be glad to get it for you."

"No, but thanks." She pointed to a leather satchel. "That was it."

"Okay, well…" He smoothed the front of his hair, pulling his hand toward his ponytail. "I should get going." Vicki started to rise, but he held her off. "No need to walk me to the door."

"Thank you so much for helping out," she said. "I owe you one."

He reached for his overnight bag. "No you don't. Just give the girls a hug from me in the morning."

"Will do."

He nodded to the redhead, then turned his gaze to Sarah. "Bye," he said, his eyes locking intimately with hers.

She brushed imaginary lint from her pants, felt her heartbeat skip and stumble. Why did she have to lose her breath every time he looked at her? Why couldn't she remain cool and calm, sophisticated like most California women?

"Bye, Adam." She gave him a shaky smile.

"Yeah. See you." He headed for the door, opened it, then closed it quietly behind him.

Sarah found the breath she had lost, let it fill her lungs. She waited a few minutes, giving Adam time to make it to his Jeep. She wanted to be sure he was he gone before she started down the steps to her own apartment.

Glancing at her watch, she checked the time, watching the second hand make its hasty sweep. "I should get going, too. Give you a chance to relax."

"Oh, no you don't." Vicki placed a firm hand on her knee, holding her in place. "You're not going anywhere until you tell me what's going on between you two."

"Going on?" She shrugged, tried to make light of her attraction to Adam. "Nothing's going on. We're just friends."

"Right." The other woman struck an austere pose. "And I'm the Queen of England. Come on, girl, 'fess up. If Adam had stayed much longer, the windows would have fogged. I know sexual tension when I see it."

Sexual tension. Even the phrase made Sarah warm. Excited. Confused. Her emotions swirled around the room, closing the walls, boxing her in. "Do you think we could step outside? Maybe have this chat on the balcony?" She needed air, a cool evening breeze to take away the heat.

"Sure." Vicki popped up, grinned and began pulling pins out of her hair, dislodging the professional twist. "Go take a seat out there, and I'll meet you in a minute. I've got to get out of these clothes."

Vicki went to her bedroom, and Sarah opened the drapes and walked onto the balcony. Standing near the rail, she gazed out at the city. The San Fernando Valley looked pretty from above, lights twinkling as far as the eye could see.

Which light was Adam's? she wondered. Was he home yet? Feeding the cats that purred at his feet?

Sarah closed her eyes and felt the wind touch her face—softly, ever so softly, like a lover's tender kiss. The air was cool but the heat remained. It was inside her, warming her blood, igniting her cells, making her think of him.

She opened her eyes and moved away from the rail. Sitting in a patio chair by a tiny glass table, she waited for Vicki to join her. Maybe talking about her feelings would help.

The other woman came onto the balcony wearing jeans and an oversize T-shirt. She sat in the other chair and drew her knees up, curls rioting around her face. She cocked her head, sent Sarah a woman-to-woman smile. "Well?"

"Adam said that he wanted me," she admitted, frowning a little.

"And that's bad?"

"No, not really. I mean, I told him that I wanted him, too."

"So, why were you two acting so strange? Sounds to me like you got it out in the open."

"It was awkward." Sarah turned to study the city lights, watch them sparkle against the night. "But that was my fault. I could barely look at him the next day. I've never said anything like that to someone before."

"You're kidding, right?"

"No." She turned back. "He's the first man I've wanted that badly. I'm still a virgin, Vicki."

"Oh, my." The redhead blinked, pushed a mass of curls away from her eyes. "That's not what I expected to hear. Most women your age…" Her words trailed, then resumed with an obvious question. "What made you wait so long?"

"My traditional upbringing. My mother had this long talk with me about saving myself for the right man."

"And you think Adam might be the one?"

"Yes, but there's more to it. Part of the reason I waited so long was to avoid an attachment." And now her heart was betraying her. She knew men weren't always what they appeared to be, yet Adam seemed so perfect. So gallant. So noble. "I want him, Vicki, but I'm afraid of taking that first step." Because once she did, there would be no turning back.

The redhead squinted. "Your virginity shouldn't be an issue, Sarah. First time or not, there's still the possibility of an attachment. Most women don't have sex for the sake of entertainment. It means something to us."

"You think I waited too long?"

"No, but you can't protect your heart forever. Eventually you have to take a chance. If you don't, you'll be alone for the rest of your life."

She let out the breath she'd been holding. "Deep down I know you're right, but I'm still confused."

"So what are you going to do?"

Suddenly pensive, Sarah glanced up at the sky. The moon was nearly full, a silver ball lighting up the valley. "I don't know," she said, wondering how it would feel to give herself to Adam, to feel his weight against her body, to lift her hips and take him deep inside.

"I just don't know," she said again, her voice blending quietly into the night.

Sarah entered her apartment, grateful she had left a low light burning. Looking around, she wished she had a companion, a cat maybe, a frisky little creature that would be happy to see her. As it was, her home seemed much too quiet.

Unsure of what to do with herself, she turned on the TV for background noise and unbuttoned her blouse. A long, soothing bath was her remedy for just about everything, including bouts of loneliness. The scent of the body oil she favored combined with a tub of warm water usually managed to lull her into a peaceful kind of solitude.

Sarah filled the tub and removed the rest of her clothing. Standing in front of the mirror, she pinned her hair up. With a sigh, she immersed herself in water.

And thought about Adam.

As she slid the washcloth over her body, she imagined his hands—those long, masculine fingers—caressing, touching her in erotic places. Her breasts, her belly, between her thighs. She imagined him leaning over her, their lips meeting, tasting—the kiss openmouthed and carnal.

Tender. Passionate.

Rising a short time later, she reached for a towel and wrapped it around herself. For a reason she couldn't quite explain, she didn't dry her body. Instead she went into her bedroom and sat on the edge of the bed.

Maybe she wanted the air to dry her skin, absorb the heat she was feeling. Sarah tilted her head, pushed away a strand of hair falling onto her shoulder.

Her closet door was open, displaying a simple wardrobe—A-line dresses, functional blouses, serviceable slacks. White, beige, a touch of mint green, a scatter of denim.

The red serpent stood out like a neon sign. Like cherries in the snow. Sex with a long, lean warrior—a dragon slayer.

Striking. Mouthwatering. Forbidden.

He wanted her to seduce him. But could she? And if she did, would she lose her heart? Would she look into his eyes and see her future?

Maybe, but it didn't matter, because Vicki was right. Sarah couldn't hide from attachments for the rest of her life. And Adam wouldn't hurt her. He was kind and decent and strong, a man who respected women, who wanted a family someday.

And wasn't that what her mother had meant by the right man? Adam had all the old-fashioned qualities Sarah admired.

Yes, she thought. She was going to make love. Tonight. With Adam.

With shaky hands, she dried her damp skin and reached for the dress. This wasn't a mistake, she assured herself, taking a deep, cleansing breath. She wasn't a Victorian virgin, nor was she naive. She had lived a cautious life, judging men with a keen, realistic eye.

Unzipping the dress, she stepped into it, allowing the satin to slide over bare flesh. Her hair came next. She released the pins and brushed it to a glossy sheen. It fell to her waist in a heavy blue-black curtain.

Because she wasn't overly skilled at applying cosmetics, she added subtle touches, hoping to soften strong Cherokee features. A coat of mascara lengthened her lashes and a copper-colored blush, flecked with a shimmering powder, highlighted her cheeks. On her mouth, she wore a natural infusion of Jamaica flowers, rosewater and cocoa butter. Sarah smiled. The ruby stain felt as sinful as being naked under a satin dress.

She dumped the contents of her purse onto the bed and placed her wallet and keys into a gold mesh bag. On her feet she wore gold sandals. Both were simple summer items, but tonight they looked exotic.

Reaching behind her, she realized she hadn't finished zipping the dress or latching the tiny hooks. Fumbling, she gave up. She was going to remove the garment anyway.

To keep herself calm, she sucked on a fruit-flavored candy and breathed a gust of sweetened air.

Cherries in the snow. The image came back like a sleek, sensual temptation. She couldn't turn back now. She wanted him far too much.

Arriving at Adam's house, she parked and sat behind the wheel for a long, drawn-out moment. The tree-lined street was quiet, the nearly full moon shining high in the sky.

Finally she went to his front door and rang the bell, convincing herself there was nothing to be nervous about.

He didn't answer right away, but when he did, her heart leaped for her throat. His hair was loose, his chest bare. And on his hips, a pair of drawstring pajama bottoms rode just below his navel.

Instantly she knew she had gotten him out of bed.

He pushed a stray lock of hair away from his face. She couldn't have imagined his hair more beautiful than it was. Rich and brown, it fell to his shoulders, as smooth and touchable as mink. Suddenly she became overly aware of being naked under the form-fitting dress.

"Sarah." He stared at her. "I can't believe you're here."

When he stepped away from the door in a silent invitation, she entered the house and stood near a wall, unsure of how to proceed.

A cat circled her feet, rubbing its sleek fur against her legs. It was the mama cat, she realized. The white one expecting a litter.

Sarah didn't move, and neither did Adam.

"You look incredible," he said.

"Thank you."

A breeze swept through the room, and she saw that the windows were open, white sheers billowing like a seductive ghost. The house was quiet, with shadows streaking across hardwood floors. The area rug in front of a tiny gas fireplace presented a wash of pale color in the dim light.

"I've never done this before," she said.

"Gone to a man's house in the middle of the night?"

"Yes. No. I was talking about sex."

He came toward her and stopped when they were inches apart, his gaze riveted to hers. "This will be your first time?"

She nodded. "Are you surprised?"

"Yes." He lifted a hand, brushed her cheek. "But—" He paused, and then frowned a little.

Nervous, she studied his troubled expression. Was he going to refuse to be with her? Send her away? "Is that a problem?"

"No. I'm honored, sweet Sarah, that you want it to be me. But I—"

"Shhh." She pressed a finger to his lips, warmed by his concern. Even though Sarah told herself the old ways no longer mattered, virginity was revered in her culture. A traditional Cherokee man would consider her offering a gift.

They were almost touching, the space between them filled by the mewling cat. "I'm naked underneath," she told him, her nipples grazing the satin. "This is your seduction, Adam." And his chivalry made it even more exciting. More meaningful.

His breath hitched, the pulse at his neck jumping. "Sarah—"

"Tell me about your fantasy. Tell me how this scene plays out."

He closed his eyes, opened them a second later. "I can't."

Because of her virginity, Sarah thought. And because he was struggling to control the primal urges she saw brewing in his eyes.

"Then do it, Adam. Make it happen."

That seemed to be more than he could bear. Pushing the dress from her body, he let it slide to the floor. Cool air shocked her skin, and then his hands were on her, warm and erotic.

Slowly, ever so slowly, he backed her against the wall, and an immediate thrill, an inexperienced fear rushed through her. She could feel his sex, hard and heavy, through the lightweight sleepwear.

The cat had vanished, so she knew the purring she heard was rising from her own throat.

Sarah couldn't describe the sensation of being pinned against a wall, his mouth holding her captive, sucking gloriously on an aching nipple.

Reaching into his hair, she grabbed hold.

He kept moving lower, that determined, wet tongue sliding over bare skin. When he dropped to his knees and looked up at her, she touched his cheek.

There was no time to be shy, to glance away timidly. He told her to watch, and she did, her gaze fixed on his handsome face.

He loved her, deeply, thoroughly, allowing her to feel like

a woman—a twenty-four-year-old seductress. Beautiful, cherished, lusted after.

She climaxed against his mouth, shattered like glass—edgy, sexy shards of colored glass. She didn't care if she was coming apart, losing pieces of herself, because soon the glass melted into wet, syrupy waves.

Sarah rode the current, the world spinning around her. And when it ended, all she could do was tremble and whisper his name.

Adam rose to his feet and held her next to his beating heart. She buried her face against his neck, felt the warmth of his skin, the silky length of his hair.

"Lie down with me," he said.

She accepted his hand, and he led her to his unmade bed. Everything, including the summer air, seemed fresh and crisp. A cool, herbal scent drifted in from the garden. Even his sheets smelled like the wind, the grass and the trees. Or maybe it was him—this natural healer with magic in his touch.

His kiss felt like enchantment, a sensual bewitching. And his body…

She roamed his chest, sliding her hands over muscle and sinew. Catching the drawstring on his pajama bottoms, she tugged. He accommodated her, shifting his hips as she removed the cotton barrier. And when he was naked, she slid her hand between his thighs.

The sound he made, the rough vulnerability, the catch in his breath, gave her power. He was battling to hold on, struggling not to plunge into her hard and deep. His blood was swimming, she thought. Pulsing through his veins in fiery bursts.

"Adam?"

"Not yet," he said. "Not this fast."

She looked up and met his gaze, and what she saw melted her.

Tenderness. So much tenderness.

"I don't want to hurt you," he said.

"You won't."

He settled his long, fluid body next to hers. Sarah studied the emotion on his face, knowing she couldn't stop the need between them, the closeness, the attachment.

"I'm so glad I waited," she said, sighing when he skimmed her cheek. He looked strong and virile, a dragon slayer with a kind and tender heart.

A man capable of capturing a woman's lonely soul.

Seven

Adam inhaled the fragrance of her skin, her hair, the scent of woman and flowers, the sweet, spicy aphrodisiac that made his blood tingle.

He slid his hands over her waist, down the curve of her hips. And then he closed his eyes, his conscience troubling him once again. How could he do this? How could he make love to her without telling her the truth?

Adam opened his eyes and saw her looking up at him. Because this mattered, he thought, brushing her lips in a tender kiss. This moment, this feeling. She had offered him a gift—a sweet, beautiful seduction. And he couldn't stop the passion, the need building between them.

Sarah arched her back, and he tongued her nipple. Her breasts were small and round, sweetly inviting. The darkness of her areolas fascinated him, the color deep and rich, like red earth touched by the sun.

She caressed him, too. Ran her palms over his shoulders, across his back, pulling him closer. Craving more, he pressed his belly to hers, felt that smooth, slick rush of flesh against flesh, limb against limb.

Adam straddled her, and she looked up at him. With silent anticipation, they watched each other, hearts pounding. Reaching into the night stand, he removed a foil packet.

She helped him put the condom on, their fingers brushing.

''Take me inside,'' he whispered when they were safe.

She stroked his face, lifted her hips and welcomed him.

Heat, moisture—that feminine tightness that made men crave this incredible feeling poured over him. And then there was resistance, just a little, just enough to remind him that he was her first.

He paused, lowered himself to nuzzle her cheek and pushed deeper. She turned her head and kissed him, took his tongue as he took her virginity.

Expecting her to tense or gasp in pain, he stopped and waited, giving her time to adjust to the hardness, the heaviness, the discomfort he assumed she would feel.

They weren't kissing anymore. They were staring into each other's eyes, their bodies joined in stillness.

It was, Adam thought, the most intimate moment of his life.

''It doesn't hurt,'' she said, a smile playing on her gorgeous mouth. ''It feels good.''

That smile, those ruby-stained lips, were nearly his undoing. He pushed himself deeper and rocked their bodies, making them both warm, wet and wondrous.

A mild breeze blew over the bed and stirred earthy scents throughout the room. Her skin was scented, too. And her hair, the flowing curtain of Cherokee hair. The unmistakable blend of cloves and carnations rose from it, seducing him.

Sweet, sweet Sarah. He couldn't get enough. Not nearly enough.

He could feel her desire, feel it building and swaying, turning into hot, fresh need. It flashed through him like lightning, a bolt as electrifying as a frayed wire.

They kissed. They danced. They made love. She moved

with him, stroke for stroke, finding his rhythm, becoming one with him.

He thought he heard her gasp, thought she was climaxing when the first shudder hit him. But he couldn't be sure. He was too far gone, steeped much too deeply in Sarah and sex. Her legs were wrapped so tightly around him, he couldn't think, couldn't focus on anything but the intensity of his release.

Afterward, he fell into her arms, and she stroked his sweat-slicked back and held him. Neither spoke, but their bodies were still joined, so words didn't seem necessary.

Adam closed his eyes. The moment drifted like the wind, as fresh and serene as the evening air. Flowers bloomed in her scent, in her long, silky hair. He turned his head and kissed her neck, deciding he could sleep there, his body buried deep within hers.

She shifted beneath him, and he lifted his head to look at her.

With her ebony hair spilling over the pillow, and her eyes as dark as the night, he thought she was the most beautiful woman in the world. And tonight she was his.

His lover. His lady.

She shifted again, so he released her from his weight, already missing the intimacy. Climbing out of bed, he headed to the adjoining bathroom. He removed the protection and discarded it, thinking condoms were a necessary nuisance. After cleaning himself, he brought Sarah a fresh washcloth, dampened with warm water.

"I thought you might need this." He knew there were spots of blood on the sheets, possibly a little on her inner thighs.

"Thank you."

He crawled back into bed beside her, and because she held the washcloth as though embarrassed to use it in front of him, he took it from her and slid it between her legs, dabbing gently.

"Are you sore?" he asked.

"No, not really. But that still feels good. Soothing."

Adam liked the idea that he was her first. He supposed it

was a macho way to feel, but it made his past seem cleaner somehow.

His past. His deception. He had to tell her.

"May I use your bathroom?"

He blinked, tried not to frown. "Of course."

She rose, taking the damp cloth with her. He couldn't tell her now, not on the heels of lovemaking. Adam gave in to the frown. So when? When would he bare his guilty soul?

A few minutes later, Sarah returned, a towel covering her nakedness. She sat on the edge of the bed, jet-black hair spilling down her back. In the morning, he decided. He would tell her in the morning.

He touched her shoulder. "Will you stay the night?"

"I can't." She turned to look at him. "I didn't bring anything with me."

"Like what?"

She laughed a little. "Pajamas, a toothbrush. You know, things a person might need."

"I have one of those travel toothbrushes that's never been opened. You can use that. And you can sleep in one of my pajama tops. I only wear the bottoms anyway."

Color rose to her cheeks. "What about underwear?"

He managed a lopsided grin. "Boxers?"

She returned his humored smile. "Okay."

He provided the necessary items, and she dressed in front of him, looking a little shy. They climbed into bed and cuddled, the way new lovers often did.

And when she fell asleep in his arms, Adam closed his eyes and inhaled the fragrance of her skin, wishing morning would never come.

The light of dawn was gray, dim and shadowy, like a poltergeist peeking through the curtains. Adam had already showered, dressed and brushed his teeth, but Sarah looked beautifully rumpled. The sheets were tangled around her legs, and her hair spilled over the pillowcase like rain.

He stood beside the bed, too guilty to give her an impulsive kiss, a good-morning nuzzle.

She squinted and sat up. "I can't believe I have to work today."

"I know. Me, too. But we have plenty of time for tea. Breakfast, too, if you're hungry." Although he couldn't possibly eat, depriving her of food didn't seem fair.

"Tea's fine."

"Then go ahead and freshen up, and I'll make it."

"Thanks." She sent him a sleepy smile. "Do you have some sweats or something I could borrow? I hate to wear that dress home."

"Sure." He pointed to the chest of drawers. "Just help yourself." A more experienced woman would have prepared herself for an overnight seduction. She would have brought a change of clothes, undergarments, toiletries.

Adam left Sarah alone and headed for the kitchen. After selecting a lemongrass tea, he tore several mint leaves from a windowsill plant, then set the water on to boil.

When she entered the room twenty minutes later, a fragrant brew steeped in the dragon teapot. On this gloomy morning, he'd decided to make use of the souvenir she'd chosen for him.

He stood at the counter, and she came up behind him and put her arms around his waist. Turning, he gave into the need to hold her, hugging her close.

Maybe she wouldn't react as strongly as he feared. Maybe he was worrying for nothing.

They separated, and she poured her tea and reached for the honey. He watched, taking note of how much sweetener she used. Suddenly her habits mattered, little things couples learned about each other.

She wore a pair of his sweatpants and a plain white T-shirt. The gray pants were rolled at the waist, and her budding nipples were slightly visible through the thin shirt. She had never looked prettier.

Adam led her to the living room, and they sat on a leather sofa the cats had clawed. He glanced up at the scratching post and saw Cameo sleeping in one of the cubbyholes. Darrin snoozed nearby, and Samantha and Tabitha were curled in a chair by the fireplace. No one seemed to mind that a woman was occupying his time, but maybe they sensed how special she was. The last woman Adam dated hadn't been partial to cats.

"What are you thinking about?" she asked.

"How much I like you." And how much he hated to spoil the companionable quiet between them. "Sarah, there's something I need to tell you."

She leaned forward. "You look so serious."

"It's a serious subject." He placed his cup on the coffee table, forming the dreaded words. "I used to have a drinking problem. Years ago, when I was a teenager."

Stunned, Sarah felt as if she'd been kicked. In the heart. With steeled-toed boots. The pain was so fierce she had to catch her breath. She'd trusted this man. This noble, kind, perfect…fraud. "A drinking problem? What's that? A sugar-coated way of saying you're an alcoholic?"

"I've been sober for eleven years."

Somehow that didn't matter right now. What mattered was that she had become emotionally and physically involved with a man who had the same disease as her father. "How convenient that you waited until *after* I slept with you to tell me."

"I tried to tell you last night. That's why I hesitated, that's why—"

"Damn you." She gripped the armrest. Even his chivalry was fake. Somehow that hurt even more. "You had plenty of opportunities to come clean, long before last night." She had confided in Adam, told him things about her childhood she had never admitted to anyone. And he had listened, never saying a word.

"I'm so sorry." He reached for his cup, set it back down again. "I couldn't bear to spoil what was happening between us, and I was afraid you would overreact. I'm not like your dad, Sarah. I'm sober, and I don't have the slightest desire to drink. It was just something associated with my youth."

And he was in denial if he thought he was immune, that it could never strike him again. "The trigger could be out there,

Adam. A reason, an excuse, that would make you want to drink again.''

"No way. It's not like that with me. It was a teenage addiction.''

She couldn't believe she was having this conversation with a man she'd made love with. She wanted to cry, to call herself a fool and him a bastard. All the sensuality, the warmth, the closeness from last night felt like a slap in the face.

"I'm sorry," he said again. "I've been so guilty about keeping this from you. To some degree, I understand what you went through with your dad. My parents had a hell of a time with me.''

One of the cats mewled and stretched, then found its way onto Adam's lap. He stroked its fur absently. Sarah watched him, blocking out images of his hands, those strong, skilled hands, caressing her body.

Unwilling to sit next to him, she took the chair opposite the couch.

"It started during my sophomore year," he said, as she shifted in her seat. "We moved, so I had to switch schools.''

Sarah wanted to say she didn't care, but a part of her needed to hear the details, needed to hear him say them out loud. She couldn't walk away until she knew every last bit of the truth. He owed her that much.

He continued, frowning as he talked. "It was a strange time for me. I had matured, you know, getting taller and broader. Better looking, I suppose, and girls at the new school noticed me." The cat slept on his lap, loyal and serene. "Popular girls," he added. "The really pretty ones the jocks usually claim.''

The betrayal stabbing Sarah's heart came back tenfold. Pretty girls. This wasn't what she wanted to hear. "So how did that lead to drinking?''

"I got invited to the in-crowd parties, and I wanted to fit in. No one pressured me, but everyone else was doing it. And it felt good hanging out with the popular kids.''

"So you overindulged?''

"Yeah. And it was so unlike me, such a contradiction to

how I had been in the past. But I was overflowing with testosterone and going through a rebellious period. Suddenly I was tired of doing homework and abiding by my parents' rules.''

Sarah couldn't relate. Her teenage years had been spent trying to keep her father from adding vodka to his orange juice in the morning and blubbering lame apologies at night. She had craved the normalcy Adam's parents had provided, the parental discipline that had been their right.

"At first I only drank on weekends," he said. "And I would come home after my mom and dad were already in bed.''

She took a long, aching breath. "When did your parents figure out what was going on?''

"When it progressed. When I got caught swiping a pint of whiskey from a local market." He looked up from the cat. "My folks had been nagging me about my flippant attitude and the hours I was keeping, but they didn't know I was drinking before school." He rolled his shoulders, his voice tight. "But then I wasn't stumbling around drunk. Most of the time I was just catching a buzz to get through the day.''

The image he'd painted made her ill, but she continued to listen.

"My parents threatened to send me away to one of those schools for troubled teens. But instead, I agreed to see a drug-and-alcohol counselor and participate in family therapy. I was sure I could con my way through that.''

"And did you?''

"Not really, no. My counselor wasn't easily fooled. And by then, neither were my parents.''

She thought about all the times her father had duped her. "I'm glad your mom and dad didn't let you take advantage of them.''

"I know. But I did change. Eventually I sobered up for good, and I began looking forward to college, to making something of myself. Holistic medicine was a natural transition. I needed to live a clean life, and I was already experimenting with herbal remedies." He trapped her gaze. "I haven't taken a drink in over eleven years, Sarah. And I'll never go down that road again. I'm not a rebellious teenager anymore.''

How could he be so sure? Plenty of alcoholics went through long periods of sobriety. There was no guarantee.

''I have to go. I don't want to be late for work.'' She stood, wishing she wasn't wearing his clothes. She needed to wash his scent from her body, push away the lingering memory of his tenderness.

Once again, a man she cared about had taken advantage of her heart. Only this time, it wasn't her father. It was Adam Paige. Her supposed friend. Her handsome, attentive lover.

Five days passed, and Sarah insisted she didn't care. She hadn't contacted him, either. She didn't want a relationship with a man she couldn't trust. And it wasn't as if she was deliberately staying home, sitting by the phone. She rarely went out after work. She hadn't changed her schedule, intending to be available for another I've-been-sober-for-eleven-years apology from Adam.

Carrying her dinner into the living room, she picked up the remote control and turned on the TV. Since she couldn't concentrate on a program already in progress, she chose a music channel, hoping to immerse herself in pop tunes.

The moment she cut into her chicken, the phone rang. She stared at it, debating whether to answer it. When she finally placed her hand on the cradle, she decided that if it was Adam, she would tell him she was busy.

''Hello?''

''Sweet Sarah.''

The nickname caught her off guard, but she did her best to hold her ground. ''I wasn't expecting to hear from you. I was just getting ready to have dinner.''

''Oh. I'm sorry. I didn't mean to bother you. I just wanted to tell you that Cameo had her kittens. God, Sarah, they're so amazing.''

Once again, she was caught off guard. He sounded like a

proud papa, his husky voice filled with awe. "How many?" she asked.

"Eight. They kinda look like little rats at this point, but Cameo thinks they're pretty special."

And so did he. She suspected the cat had given birth in his room, maybe even on his bed. "Congratulations," she said.

"Thanks. Will you come by and see them?"

Suddenly, saying no didn't feel like an option. She wrapped her dinner in aluminum foil and slipped her feet into a pair of sandals. Who could refuse to visit a litter of kittens? Certainly not a woman whose empty apartment was crying out for a pet.

Adam answered the door with a cautious smile, and seeing him again set off a primitive reaction, tightening her nipples beneath a simple cotton bra. His hair was banded into a ponytail, and a blue T-shirt clung to his chest, but she knew what he looked like naked with his hair flowing over his shoulders.

"The kittens are in my room," he said.

In spite of their awkward reunion, Sarah melted. A wooden box sat in a secluded corner. But not just any box. This one had been customized with a nest of cloth strips and a makeshift curtain.

"I put this in the laundry room weeks ago, but Cameo wouldn't go near it until I moved it in here." They knelt in front of the box, and Adam opened the curtain a little more. "Sarah came to see your babies," he told the cat in a soft voice.

Cameo meowed in response, and Sarah peeked in. The new mother lay on her side, and the kittens either nursed or slept in a huddle. They came in a variety of colors, including black, white, gray and combinations thereof.

"Were they born today?"

He nodded. "I called you as soon as I knew they were all okay. I had to help a little. She had three of them so close together, that she seemed to be struggling to get to all of them in time. One of them didn't look like it was breathing, so I cleaned the membrane from its face and cut the cord." Adam sat back on his haunches. "I hated to intervene, but I didn't know what else to do. I was afraid she might reject it after that, but she didn't. She seemed grateful for the help."

"Then apparently you did the right thing. You know, I was thinking about getting a cat. A kitten." And now she wanted the one he had saved. "My house gets pretty quiet. I could use the company."

"That's great. I'd love for you to have one. In six weeks you can have the pick of the litter."

"Thank you."

So polite, she thought. So proper. His bed was a few feet away, but they were acting as though they hadn't made love, hadn't rubbed and kissed and put their hands all over each other.

"Do you want a male or a female?" he asked.

"I'm not sure," she said, wondering about the one he had saved. "I guess I can decide later."

"That's fine with me." He sent her a lopsided grin. "Because I don't have the slightest idea how to sex kittens. It's not real obvious, like with puppies."

"Or humans," she said, feeling warm.

"Yeah, them, too." His smile faded, and they stared at each other.

The secluded corner was much too confining. Their knees brushed, an innocent touch that had Sarah fumbling for something to say.

The windows were open, but nothing stirred. Nothing but the tender sounds coming from the nursery box. Kittens mewling and suckling.

"I should go," she finally managed, pulling herself to her feet.

He followed suit, but they didn't get far. They made it to the hallway before they stopped, their eyes drawn like magnets. When he moved closer, she had to tell herself to breathe.

"I thought about calling you so many times," he said, his voice tinged with emotion. "I wanted to go to your house, visit you at work. Tell you over and over again how sorry I am."

Her heart pummeled her chest. "Then why didn't you?"

"Because I was trying to give you some space."

There was less than an inch between them now, and the air she struggled to breathe was as thick and humid as a summer night. The hallway was dim and narrow, but suddenly it seemed like the most sexual place on earth. How could this be happening? How could she still be attracted to him?

"Don't ever deceive me again," she said.

"I won't."

He moistened his lips, and a shiver streaked down her spine.

"Sarah?"

"Yes?"

"Are we still friends?"

She knew she should say no. Erasing Adam from her life was the safe, sane thing to do, but she couldn't let him go. Not completely. "Yes."

"Thank you. That means a lot to me."

He skimmed her cheek, her jaw, the curve of her neck. They were close, so close their lips were nearly touching, nearly meeting in a kiss that would melt like honey and sizzle like fire.

Drawing strength from the ache in her chest, from the memory of being wounded, Sarah stepped back, away from Adam, away from the warmth, the heat, the sensuality of his caress.

No matter how much he stirred her blood, she couldn't take the chance of losing her heart, of letting him hurt her again. His past made him too much of a risk.

"We can be friends," she said. "But not lovers. What happened between us was a mistake."

No, it wasn't, Adam thought, as Sarah crossed her arms. Making love, holding each other, feeling warm and tender—that wasn't a mistake.

"I understand," he told her, knowing he couldn't push the issue. Sarah struggled with intimacy, and he had blown her trust by deceiving her. And now, he supposed, he seemed dangerous in her eyes. A Cherokee with a history of alcoholism. He had two major strikes against him, but damn it, he couldn't change his past or the Native blood running through his veins.

At least she had agreed to remain friends. Adam couldn't bear losing her for good. And if they spent enough time together, Sarah would see him for the true person he was. Wouldn't she?

"Do you want to cheat?" he asked.

"What?" She blinked, then stared at him with a confused expression.

"Cheat. You know, eat something sweet. I bought some chocolate eclairs yesterday."

"You did?" She tilted her head. "Why?"

"Just in case you decided to forgive me." And because he had fantasies about her mouth, about watching her eat something rich and creamy. He couldn't seem to get her out of his system, and his urges had been going from sinful to soft in a heartbeat.

Sex. Summer seductions. A house in the country. Dark-eyed, dark-haired babies.

All of it involved intimacy, and all of it involved making love with Sarah. The idea of needing her so badly scared him, but he couldn't let go. They deserved a chance to explore the emotions that had begun to unfold, the attachment that could make a difference in their lives.

He reached for her hand, breathed a sigh of relief when she didn't pull away. "So, are you up for a chocolate binge, sweet Sarah?"

She gave him a nervous smile. "I guess so. I mean, you already bought the eclairs. There's no point in letting them go to waste."

"Good." He led her to his kitchen, and when she stood near the window, he saw a beautiful, beguiling woman.

Her cheekbones caught the light, and her hair cascaded to her waist, as sleek and compelling as nightfall. Everything about her looked exotic, especially the shape of her eyes. They tilted at the corners, giving her a bewitching quality.

Yes, Adam thought. That was the description that fit the way he felt.

Sarah Cloud had bewitched him, lulled him into a quiet, confusing enchantment.

Eight

Sarah agreed to spend Sunday afternoon with Adam. It was their day off, and the sun shone bright and pretty. He hadn't told her what they'd be doing, but he'd said it would be a casual outing.

She sat across from him in his Jeep, the wind blowing through her hair. He drove like most Californians—fast and aggressive. There was a time when freeways made her nervous, but she had gotten used to the quick lane changes and congested traffic.

He exited on a winding off-ramp that took them into an area showcasing equestrian shops and exclusive ranch homes.

"Come on, Adam. Where exactly are we going?"

He stopped at a red light and grinned. "To look at the paint I'm going to buy."

"You ride?" She didn't know why that surprised her. He certainly looked the part with his sexy-fitting denims and golden skin.

"I've been riding since I was a kid," he said. "I had a

horse up until I got into trouble. And then, well, things sort of changed after that.''

With silent understanding, she nodded. His drinking had interfered with the simple pleasures of life. ''Where did you board your horse?'' she asked, knowing he had grown up in a suburban neighborhood.

''At a facility not far from here.''

''And is that where you're going to board this new horse?''

''Yep. For a while, anyway.'' He turned onto a street that led to the hills. ''Eventually I plan to buy my own place. As many acres as I can afford. I've always wanted to have horse property.''

They passed a fancy stylized home, displaying an attractive barn, a riding arena and a hot walker. Sarah raised her eyebrows. ''You don't plan on buying around here, do you?''

Her question made him laugh. ''Are you kidding? I have some money, but I'm not rich.'' Soon his laughter faded, his voice serious. ''I inherited a fair amount from my parents. But even with the investments I've made, it's not enough to buy a ranch in this area. We're talking millions to live here.''

A gust of warm air tousled Sarah's hair. She pushed the flyaway strands away from her face and reached for the bottled water they had brought along. ''Then where are you going to go?'' She knew there was more affordable acreage in California, even if most of it was desert.

He turned to look at her. ''I was thinking Oklahoma.''

A knot formed in her stomach. ''You've never even been there.''

He stopped in front of a large estate and killed the engine. ''I know, but it seems like the only thing I have, the place where I'm supposed to be. California hasn't felt like home for a long time, Sarah. I've stayed because I didn't know where else to go.''

''What about your job?''

''I can always find work. I'm good at what I do, and there are people who follow the holistic path everywhere. There has to be a clinic in Oklahoma that would hire me.'' He leaned his head against the seat. "I just don't think I can handle living in California much longer."

Not now that he knew he had been born in Tahlequah, she thought. Knew that he might have family in Oklahoma. "I guess taking that trip will help you decide."

"Yeah, especially if I find my mom." He skimmed her hand. "I wish you would agree to come with me. I don't want to go alone. I really need you there."

"I—" Panic welled in her chest, hard and fast and shaky. Her heartbeat stumbled and tripped, then bounced back with thundering beats. Going home scared her, and so did the fact that he had just told her that he needed her. "I can't think about this now."

"Okay." He turned to gaze out the window, his profile strong and strikingly chiseled. "It's still over a month away. I won't push you."

Because her heart was still thundering, she drank small sips of water, battling jittery nerves. "Why are we parked here? Is this where your new horse is?"

He nodded. "I gave the current owner a deposit."

"So you're paying off the balance today?"

"Yep."

He turned toward her, and she wondered if he would actually find his mother in Oklahoma. And if he did, would he discover that his alcoholism was genetic?

They exited the car and headed toward the barn. The woman who greeted them was tall and fashionably slim, with short blond hair and an aristocratic face that had been aged a little too early by the sun. She looked wealthy and well bred, a lady born to the California equestrian set.

Her name was Carol, and she was the divorced mother of two college-age daughters. Carol also appeared to find Adam attractive, but that didn't surprise Sarah because females of all ages and lifestyles were drawn to him. Unfortunately, Sarah found herself admiring him, too. He stood tall and broad-shouldered, his body hard and lean and muscular, the sun playing off his hair, highlighting various shades of brown.

The horse he had chosen, a sorrel overo paint, was as strik-

ing as the man. And it was a mare. She had expected it to be
a gelding, but Adam had bought himself a gentle-eyed female.

"We call her Cee-Cee," Carol told her. "It was our nickname for Sienna's Pride."

The mare, Sarah also learned, had belonged to Carol's oldest daughter and was primarily used as a trail horse, which
was exactly what Adam wanted.

"He'll take good care of her," she said.

Carol motioned to the stall and smiled. "Yes, I suspect he
will."

Sarah turned to find Cee-Cee nuzzling Adam's neck like a
long-lost lover. Even the horse had developed a crush on him.

Within three weeks, the kittens had grown into eight little
balls of adorable fluff. Some were developing faster than others, and Sarah's favorite, of course, was the most independent
one. She named him Groucho because he had black slashes
above his eyes that looked remarkably like big, animated eyebrows. He was also the baby Adam had saved, and that made
him even more special.

Sarah and Adam sat on the floor in his room, the kittens
stumbling around their feet. Groucho wandered in another
direction, but Cameo latched onto him and dropped him back
into the thick of things. The mama cat kept her eye on everyone, including the humans playing with her young brood.

Adam glanced up and said, "Groucho could be a girl, you
know."

"No way." She reached for her favorite kitty. "Look at
that face. This one's definitely a boy."

He grinned. "It's got nothing to do with faces, sweetheart.
It's the other end that counts."

"Smart aleck." She turned Groucho over in her palm and
rubbed his belly. The kitten batted his tiny paws in response.
"Maybe it's time we tried to figure this out. Where's that
book you bought?"

Adam made his way to the nightstand and retrieved the
book. When he returned, he flipped through the pages until
he came to the breeding section. "Determining the Sex of

Your Kittens.'' He announced, then read the paragraph to himself and regarded Groucho with a perplexed expression. ''We're supposed to elevate his tail and view him from the rear. If he's a male, his…um…area is supposed to be lower than a female's, and it says you should be able to feel his—'' he made a face only a man could make at a time like this and finished his sentence, ''—testicles.''

Biting back a smile, she handed him the kitten. ''Here. You can do that.''

''Gee, thanks.''

Groucho didn't seem to mind the examination. If anything, he looked amused. Sarah could have sworn his eyebrows waggled.

Adam's expression didn't change. During the procedure, he kept that uncomfortable look on his face. Somehow that made Groucho's comical eyebrows even funnier.

Sarah coughed to cover a giggle, and Adam shook his head.

''I'm feeling around for testes, and you're laughing.''

''Sorry. Couldn't help it.''

''Yeah, well, I'm not getting this. I think I need to compare kittens. Maybe find a female first.''

Sarah lost the battle to remain serious, and soon her giggling had Adam laughing, too. But even through their silly fit, he finally figured out what he was doing. Groucho, he discovered, was indeed a boy.

''Told you.'' Sarah beamed and kissed the top of the kitty's head. ''He's a regular little stud.''

''Yeah, I guess he is.''

The mama cat decided the visit was over when most of her babies started bumping into her, insisting it was time to nurse. Adam and Sarah rounded up the kittens and placed them in the nursery box, leaving Cameo alone with them.

''Come on,'' he said. ''Let's go fix a snack.''

They entered the kitchen, and she leaned against the counter. ''So what are we going to make?''

He washed his hands and turned back to face her. ''Fry bread.''

Sarah was startled. She had no idea Adam was familiar

with fry bread. "I don't know how to make it," she said, which was more or less the truth. She had never actually prepared it herself. And just the smell alone would remind her of the intertribal powwows her mother had loved to attend. She wasn't up for a painful trip down memory lane.

"I have a recipe," he said. "And I bought everything we need yesterday."

"As far as I know, fry bread is a Navaho dish," she said. "So if you're looking for a Cherokee experience, this isn't it."

"Really? Well, I got the recipe from a Cherokee newspaper, so that's good enough for me. Come on, Sarah. You know what a lousy cook I am. I can't do this without you."

Further argument was pointless. Adam was already gathering the ingredients. Sarah washed her hands and dried them on a paper towel, telling herself it was only a snack. It didn't have to remind her of lost dreams and faraway powwows. She could separate the past from the present.

A persistent cat meowed at the back door, so she answered the summons while Adam searched for an appropriate frying pan. She knelt on the tiny porch and placed a bowl of dry cat food on the bottom step. The feline was a war-torn tom who never came into the house. He wouldn't let anyone touch him, but he wasn't too proud to accept a free meal now and then.

She watched him, wondering if he was the father of Cameo's kittens. The tom's bluish gray coat was the color of a rain-shrouded sky. Secretly she called him Storm. The name seemed to fit this wary stray.

He looked as though he had been in a fight recently, but she knew he wouldn't allow himself to be doctored. Sarah understood his need to be alone, to choose solitude over the emotion and turmoil that came with being part of a family.

The tom studied her with knowing green eyes, and she smiled. He seemed to understand her, too. To respect her for keeping her distance, for not trying to lure him with pretty words and promises of forever.

I should have been a cat, she mused, leaving the hungry tom alone.

Going back into the house, she saw that Adam waited for her.

"Who was it?" he asked.

"The gray tom."

"How did he look?"

"A little battered. Like he's been in another fight."

A frown creased his forehead. "I know cats are independent, but that one worries me."

Trust Adam, she thought, to want to stitch the cuts, heal the bruises, give the tom a warm place to sleep. "He appears to be able to take care of himself."

"Not if a car gets him."

Sarah met Adam's gaze. Those tender brown eyes could melt a woman's heart, leave her as warm and molten as wax. He protected everyone—the dragon slayer who took in strays. Deep down she knew Adam hadn't intended to hurt her. But as much as she valued his friendship, being intimate with him still frightened her.

"Have you named him?" Adam asked, referring to the wary tom.

She tucked her hair behind her ears. This conversation was going in a direction that made her uncomfortable. She would never say Storm's name out loud. To do so would lay too much claim. "No," she lied. "Have you?"

"No, but if he knew where you lived, he would visit your house, too. They all would."

"Groucho's coming home with me, remember?" And Groucho was probably Storm's son. That gave her an attachment to the roaming tom, a bond she couldn't deny. They were almost like family. Her and Adam and the cats.

Sarah glanced at the stove. This wasn't supposed to happen. She wasn't suppose to feel this way. "I thought we were making fry bread."

He smiled and reached for her hand, drawing her closer. "We are."

The recipe was simple—flour, salt, water, baking powder and powdered milk. They measured the ingredients and mixed them into a bowl. While the oil heated, they shaped the bread.

The recipe claimed size was a matter of preference, so Adam's palm-size mounds came out bigger than Sarah's.

Standing side by side, they flattened the dough into disks, then placed them in the oil, turning each one as it browned.

Adam had flour on his chin. Sarah gave him a motherly "tsk" and brushed him clean. He grinned and rewarded her with a playful hug. He seemed so happy, so incredibly pleased to have her in his kitchen, sharing a simple but important moment of his life.

The fry bread, she supposed, made him feel more Indian. Adam wanted so desperately to belong, to be accepted into a culture that had yet to recognize him. He wasn't registered with the Cherokee Nation. Officially he wasn't a member of the Western or Eastern Band. He didn't have an enrollment number linking him to his ancestors. All he had was an aging document stating his mother's name and heritage.

"It's almost ready," he said.

Sarah turned back to the task at hand. The recipe produced four servings. Adam drained their bounty in a brown paper bag lined with napkins, and she inhaled the fried aroma.

Tea steeped in the dragon pot. It smelled wonderful, too. Man, mint and fry bread. It was, she thought, a heady combination.

A combination that seemed to wrap itself around her reluctant heart.

The following Sunday, Adam invited Sarah to Mason Ranch, the boarding facility that housed his horse.

Sarah exited Adam's Jeep and looked around. Ancient oaks offered shade and scenic trails led to a hilltop view. A roping arena sat on one side of the property, wash racks and lockers on the other. Mason Ranch was an urban-cowboy facility, catering to boots, buckles and well-worn denim.

And today, Adam fit the bill. Gorgeous Adam in a pair of slim-fitting Wranglers. Just the sight of him made her blood tingle.

He entered Cee-Cee's stall, and the paint greeted him with

friendly eyes and a bobbing head. Sarah stood on the other side of the gate and watched them.

"She probably thinks we're going for a ride," he said. "I've been taking her into the hills nearly every morning."

"You come here before work?"

He nodded and pushed against Cee-Cee, who was nudging him for attention. "You should see this place at dawn, Sarah. It's incredible."

"I'll bet it is." She pictured the sun rising over the hills like a ball of fire. "Do you hit traffic on the way back?"

"A little. But it's worth it." He lifted Cee-Cee's halter and slipped it over her head. "I cut it close, though. I have just enough time for a quick shower before I go to work." Buckling the halter, he spoke to the mare now, his voice deep but gentle. "It's not going to be like this forever. Someday we're going to have our own ranch. Aren't we, girl?"

A place in Oklahoma, Sarah thought uncomfortably. She was going to lose Adam to the world she'd left behind. Lose him? He was only supposed to be her friend, not a man she hoped to keep. "You're not moving for a while."

"Actually, I might find a place this summer." The mare's neighbor, a big bay gelding, poked his nose over the rail. Adam smiled at the curious horse and led Cee-Cee out of the stall. "I've already contacted a Realtor in Oklahoma. They're going to show me some property while I'm there." He paused, looked over at her. "I wish you would agree to take that vacation with me."

Sarah closed the gate, and they fell into step, with Adam leading the paint. She didn't want to talk about this. The day was much too nice to ruin.

They continued on the path that led to the lockers, passing a picnic area rife with benches. She decided the best course was a silent one. Rather than respond to his comment, she let it drift between them, float until it disappeared.

Cee-Cee didn't shy away from the wash rack. She allowed Adam to hitch her to a post without the slightest fuss. Sarah had pictured the mare dragging her hoofs like a stubborn child. Cee-Cee, with her gentle eyes and flashy coat, was a bit on the spoiled side.

"She really is a good horse," Sarah said.

"Yeah, she is." Turning on the hose, he let the water run for a moment. "How long has it been since you've ridden?"

"Years. Since I was a kid. Some of my friends had horses."

"Do you miss it?"

She studied the paint. "Yes, I suppose I do." It was a difficult admission to make, but she chose to be honest. Sarah had stopped riding after her mother died, and there were moments she longed for the simple pleasure of a dusty trail.

They soaped down the mare together, their clothes taking a good portion of the dirt. Cee-Cee had decided to dance after all, whinnying as she did. Sarah had to laugh. The horse wasn't spooked. The big overgrown baby was singing in the shower.

While Cee-Cee basked in the sun, Adam and Sarah dried themselves with the same towel. Watching him tackle his damp shirt, she had to tell her hormones to behave. With a Western hat dipped over his eyes, he looked sexier than lust-driven sin. All denim and all male, she thought. Muscles bunched in his arms and a buckle glinted at his waist.

"Adam?" a man's voice said. "Is that you, Paige?"

They both turned, and then Adam grinned.

"Hey, Dan. What a surprise." He clasped the other man's hand in a friendly shake. "Do you board here?"

"Sure do."

Dan was lanky and blond, with hazel eyes that crinkled when he smiled. Beside him was a young Mexican woman, very pretty and very pregnant. A little boy held her hand, his skin a light shade of brown. Sarah assumed they were a family.

Dan turned to the woman. "Angie, you remember Adam, don't you?"

She nodded and smiled. "From the league, right?"

"Yes, it's nice to see you again."

Once all of the introductions were made, Sarah learned that

Adam and Dan had played basketball on the same city league six years before. She was also told that Dan and Angie had been married forever and had named their son Jordan because Dan was a die-hard basketball fan.

Adam knelt to greet the boy. "Hey, partner. Do you ride?"

Jordan bobbed his head, tipping the cowboy hat he wore. "I ride with my daddy, and I get to hold the reins."

"Pretty cool. How old are you?"

The child held up three fingers, but said, "Four."

"He'll be four in September," his mother clarified.

"Yep." Jordan's hat teetered again. "And that's when I'm gonna be a big brother. My mom's havin' another boy. We know 'cause the doctor took a picture of him inside her tummy." The child made an expressive face and leaned into Adam. "It showed his pee-pee and everything."

"Oh, yeah?"

Adam broke into a grin and glanced up at Dan, who flashed a that's-my-kid smile back at him. Sarah and Angie just laughed.

"Do you got a horse?" Jordan asked Adam.

"Yeah. She's right over there. Do you want to meet her?"

"Sure." The three-year-old reached for Adam as if they were life-long buddies. "What's her name?"

He balanced the child with ease. "Cee-Cee. And she loves carrots. We can feed her one, okay?"

Sarah could only stand back and marvel. Jordan clung to Adam's neck while the boy's parents watched with proud smiles. Jordan already knew how to feed a horse, so Adam praised him for being such a good cowboy. Cee-Cee cooperated as well, reaching for the carrot with a delicate nibble.

They looked right together, Sarah thought. The man, the child and the big, flashy paint.

Dan finally told Jordan it was time to go home. The boy whined but agreed that his pregnant mom should take a nap. Sarah suspected Jordan would be napping before long, too. He insisted he didn't need one, but heavy eyelids indicated otherwise.

"You should barbecue with us one weekend," Angie said, extending the invitation to both Sarah and Adam.

Before they could respond, Dan chimed in. "Yeah, that would be great, except I'll bet Adam's still a health-food nut."

"That's right, I am. But I have been known to cheat." He bumped Sarah's arm and grinned.

They bantered a little more, laughing and joking. Sarah joined in, even though she felt a little strange. The other couple acted as if she and Adam were living together, as if they were on the verge of a major commitment.

But they were just friends, she thought. Friends who had been one-time lovers.

A few minutes later Jordan waved goodbye as his dad carried him to their car. The little boy's hat bobbed, as big and floppy as his grin.

Adam returned the child's wave, then leaned against a hitching post. "He's quite a kid, isn't he?"

"Yes, he is." Sarah squinted into the sun. Jordan was no longer visible. He was strapped in the back seat, tinted windows shielding him from view.

"He looks like us."

Blinking, she turned. Adam stared at her, his eyes intense. How many times had he watched her like that? So tender, so earnest.

"Us?" she all but stuttered.

"Like he could be our son."

This wasn't a conversation she wanted to have. Friends didn't imagine what their children would look like. Couples did that, people in serious relationships.

"Adam—"

He touched her cheek, his fingertips gentle. Whatever she intended to say was lost. The world stilled. She couldn't see anything but him. And the face of a dark-haired, dark-eyed child.

Their child.

"I think about it, Sarah. I think about having babies with you."

Closing her eyes, she fought the image. His words, those romantic words, pierced a part of her that already ached—the part that knew it wouldn't work.

"I think it's time to go," she said. "It's hot, and I'm tired. And..." She couldn't bring herself to talk, not here. Not beneath a blue sky and a bright yellow sun. Not with giant oaks offering quiet shade and horses whinnying for attention. It was all too beautiful to spoil.

Masking a tight expression, Adam stepped back. He should have kept silent, kept his feelings to himself. Sarah would barely look at him, and damn it, that hurt.

"I'll take Cee-Cee back to her stall."

"That's fine. I'll wait here."

Untying the horse, he led her across the dirt and down a tidy row of pipe stalls. In the distance, the hills rose to the sky, edging the heavens in a wash of color, a setting that seemed almost surreal.

"What should I do?" he asked the paint. "How do I get her out of my system?"

Cee-Cee nuzzled him as he opened the gate, and he had to chuckle. "Offering to take her place, are you?"

Why did he have to fall for a female who didn't want him? "They chase me," he told the horse. "Women actually chase me." But not Sarah. Whenever he tried to close the gap between them, she widened it even more.

Unbuckling Cee-Cee's halter, he found himself being nudged. The mare poked and prodded, and he realized he was being patted down for carrots. "And here I thought you loved me." He reached into his pocket and handed her the last bite.

When he exited the stall, Cee-Cee's neighbor tossed his head, sending his mane flying. The gelding was courting her, Adam thought, showing off proud and pretty.

"Don't bother," he said under his breath, feeling cynical and hurt and much too male.

Sarah stood right where he'd left her. She gazed at the sky, and he wondered what she was thinking. Maybe it was over between them. Maybe this was it. The subject that would pull them apart for good.

Babies. The possibility of a future. Something deeper and more meaningful than friendship.

Damn it. His heart ached something fierce. "Let's go," he said.

They climbed into the Jeep without uttering a single word. The freeway was busy, so he concentrated on the SUV in front of him, shifting gears when the traffic came to a blinding halt.

"Great," he muttered. He couldn't wait to get the hell out of the city.

Sarah tucked a strand of hair behind her ear. "There's probably an accident up ahead."

"Yeah, probably." He couldn't see anything but a sea of cars and graffiti on an overhead pass. The concrete jungle on a typical day.

They moved at a snail's pace, but once they reached the holdup, Adam's breath lodged in his throat. There was indeed an accident, a collision on the other side of the road. He caught a glimpse of flashing lights and mangled metal, emergency vehicles and clean white stretchers.

Turning away, he thought about the plane crash that had taken his parents' lives. He wanted to reach for Sarah's hand, hold it tightly in his. Life was too short to lose what mattered. Adam missed his parents, missed the loving, caring people who had raised him as their son. They hadn't told him about the adoption, but they had seen him through the roughest time of his life.

"It looks bad," Sarah said.

"Yeah, it does."

He was grateful when the traffic picked up and they left the accident behind. He didn't want to dwell on funerals and cemeteries and sympathy cards you wished you didn't have to open.

Sarah's sprawling apartment complex sat in the heart of the Valley. Adam entered through the security gate and parked in a visitor's spot. He noticed a fenced playground beside the clubhouse. Kids were welcome and so were dogs, as long as they weighed under thirty pounds. There were two swimming pools and lots of restrictions. He wondered if Sarah ever felt stifled.

"Do you want to come in?" she asked.

He hesitated, simply because he hadn't expected an invitation. "Are you sure you're up for company?"

She brushed his hand. "We need to talk, Adam."

"All right." Something akin to fear gripped his belly. Was this it? he wondered. The talk that would end his chance of winning her over? The we-shouldn't-see-each-other-anymore speech? Our relationship is getting too complicated? I don't want to have babies with a guy who used to drink?

They walked to her door in silence, activity stirring around them. Most of her neighbors either barbecued on their tiny patios or headed to the closest pool, towels and suntan lotion in tow.

Once they were inside, Sarah offered him a cold drink. Still a little sweaty from grooming the horse, he accepted a tall glass of cranberry juice, finishing it in several long swallows.

He sat at her dining room table, waiting for the ax to fall. She sat across from him, sipping her juice.

He wanted to jump up, stretch his legs, roll his shoulders. His muscles were tight, his body on edge. He needed a shower, a therapeutic spray of warm water to take his mind off what was happening.

"So?" he said, meeting her gaze head-on. The sooner this ended, the sooner he could go home, close his eyes and try to forget.

"What you said earlier—" she paused to take another sip, ice cubes crackling in her glass. "It was nice, Adam. A nice thing to say."

Stunned, he blinked, losing sight of her for an instant. "Really? I thought it upset you."

"It scared me. And it still does. We're not supposed to have these kind of feelings for each other. We're not supposed to fantasize about what our children will look like."

"Why not?" He leaned into the table, wishing he could

touch her. "We're young and healthy and single. It's normal. Men and women get attached. That's what life is about."

"But it won't work." She shook her head, and he wondered if she was trying to shake off her emotions.

"Why won't it work, Sarah?"

She pushed away her juice, leaving a streak of moisture across the glass tabletop. "I promised myself a long time ago that I would never get involved with an alcoholic."

"And I promised myself I would never drink again. It's not a problem in my life anymore, and it shouldn't come between us."

"You're obsessed with Oklahoma," she countered.

He gave in to the urge to stand, to stretch his legs and roll his shoulders. "It's not an obsession. I might have family there. And I've been asking you to come with me."

She set her jaw. "I can't go back there."

"Yes, you can." He sat down again, only this time he took the chair closest to hers. "You need to go back. For yourself. For us. For your dad."

"My dad?"

She flinched, and he knew he had hit a raw nerve. "Yeah. The man you haven't seen or spoken to in over six years. It's time to face him, don't you think? Tell him what a mess he made of things."

Her jaw was still set, stiff and tighter than a drum. "And what good would that do?"

"It might give you some peace of mind. And it might restore a little pride in your heritage. You've been blaming a whole nation of people for one man's mistakes. Your dad ruined it for you. And now you're ruining it for us." He inhaled, let the air out slowly. "Didn't you see that accident today? Damn it, life is too short to waste. Your mother is gone. My parents are dead. Who do we have left?" He answered his own question, his heart aching for both of them. "I'll tell you who. The people who gave me up for adoption and the father who disappointed you. They're it. They're all we've got."

She didn't respond. Instead she just stared at him, her eyes watery. And when her mouth finally moved, her words came out soft and broken, like a jagged whisper. "He sends me letters."

Adam didn't need to ask who she meant. He knew she was talking about her dad. Reaching for her hand, he felt it tremble in his. "What do they say?"

Her fingers curled around his. "I don't know. I've never opened them."

"Oh, Sarah." Sweet, confused Sarah. "You have to read them."

"They're probably full of phony promises."

"It doesn't matter. You still have to read them."

"I will," she said. "But I don't want to do it alone. Will you stay with me? Be here when I open them?"

"Of course I will." He moved closer, breathing in the scent of her hair. They might be two lonely people, adults struggling to survive without a family, but today, they had each other.

She closed her eyes, and for the longest time, they sat in her dining room, simply holding hands. For now, he thought, it was enough.

Nine

Sarah squeezed his hand. It frightened her to need someone so badly, yet she couldn't deny that at this life-altering moment, she needed a companion.

Adam. She needed Adam.

How many times had she stared at those letters, trying to garner the courage to read them?

She took a deep breath, knowing there was no point in prolonging the inevitable. "They're in my closet." Rising, she invited him to join her.

They entered her room, and he sat on the edge of her bed. Hesitating, she stood by the door and looked at him. His jeans were slightly soiled, his hair matted from the hat he had worn earlier. A faint sunburn marked his cheeks and the bridge of his nose.

"Is it because I'm Cherokee?" she asked.

He cocked his head. "What do you mean?"

"Is that why you haven't let me go? Being Indian is so important to you. And I'm the only Cherokee you know."

A frown creased his brow. "How can you say something like that? How could you even think it?" He pounded on his chest, then spread his hand over it. "I haven't let you go because you live inside me. Right here, all the time."

Dizzy, she teetered, then held onto the doorknob for support. What he described sounded so tender, so passionate. So real. "The Cherokee have a saying—" she met his gaze, her pulse quickening. "They say that when you care about someone, that person walks in your soul."

"Is that what's happening to me?" he asked.

"I don't know." Maybe it was happening to both of them. Maybe they walked in each other's souls. Walked so deeply, there was no way out. "I shouldn't have brought this up."

"It's okay." He watched her with intensity. "It scares me, too, Sarah."

Were they talking about love? The emotion she'd feared all along? "I was just feeling insecure. You know, about the Cherokee thing. I had no right to accuse you of being so shallow." She glanced at the top of her closet. The door was open, beckoning her to come closer. "It's those letters, I guess."

He nodded. "I understand."

She stepped forward, reached for a small box. Removing the envelopes, she placed them on the bed beside Adam. Her father's handwriting caught her attention. She closed her eyes, then opened them, knowing she couldn't blink away this moment. The letters were bundled together with a rubber band. Adam picked them up and studied them.

"How did he get your address?"

"I kept in touch with a high-school friend for a while. She must have given it to him."

He removed the rubber band. She knew the oldest postmark was from two years before, the most recent just several months ago. There were six letters in all.

Adam indicated the return address. "I've never heard of this town."

"Hatcher is a small community, between Tulsa and Tahlequah. It's quiet, a little off the beaten path. I've passed through it, but never stopped.''

"And that's where your dad lives now?''

"So it seems.''

He handed her the oldest letter, suggesting she read them in chronological order.

She took it and tore the seal, feeling like Pandora opening that box. What if this turned out to be a mistake? What if it just ended up drawing her back into a world of pain?

Dear Sarah....

The text was short and fairly simple. He apologized in the first sentence, told her he had stopped drinking in the second.

"I've heard all of this before.'' She finished reading it and gave it to Adam. Opening the next envelope, her heart sank. In this note, her father admitted that he had slipped up and taken a drink, but he was going to try harder.

From there, the letters continued in the same tone. He continued to apologize, telling her how sorry he was for letting her down, for being an irresponsible parent. He loved her, he claimed, loved her so much.

"He seems sincere.'' Adam re-bundled the stack. "And it appears he's been sober for almost two years now. He only screwed up that once. Plus he's been attending meetings ever since.''

"So he says.'' Sarah fingered the rubber band. It could have been fastened around her heart, constricting the beats. "I want to believe him, but these letters don't prove a thing. He's lied about being sober before.'' And he'd told her that he loved her before, too. So many times. "They're just words.''

"No, they're not. They're his feelings. His struggle. He misses you, Sarah. He wants to do the right thing.''

"You're so trusting.''

"I've been there. I remember what it felt like to disappoint the people who loved me. Your dad deserves a chance to prove himself.''

She gazed at Adam. His adoptive father was dead. And his

biological father was a nameless, faceless man he hoped to meet someday.

"I have to go to Oklahoma, don't I?"

He smoothed her hair, brushed a strand from her cheek. "It's the only way to know if he's telling the truth. If he really is sober."

Forcing air through her lungs, she fought to temper the rising panic. "And if he isn't?"

"Then we'll deal with it. Together."

Together. The word melted over her like a balm. She leaned into Adam, and he held her. Close. So very close. He understood how much she needed his support.

She nuzzled his neck, and he stroked her back.

"Will you stay here tonight?" she asked.

He leaned back to look at her, to touch her cheek. "You know I will."

They stared at each other, and while silence engulfed the room, Sarah told herself she couldn't keep punishing Adam for his teenage rebellion. Eleven years of sobriety was a long time.

"I have to go to my place to get a change of clothes," he said finally. "And I could use a shower, too."

"You can shower here."

He sent her a seductive smile. "With you?"

"Yes." She wanted to hold him, feel his nakedness against hers.

They made it to his house within twenty minutes. He opened the front door and a wall of "meows" greeted him. One eager tabby jumped straight into his arms. He laughed and stroked its mottled coat. "I guess everybody's hungry."

No, Sarah thought. It wasn't food they were after. It was him.

And she couldn't blame them. She wanted to be near him, too.

Adam gave the cats canned food. He spoiled them, she supposed, but all of them had come from the streets. They deserved to know that someone cared. As a youth, Sarah had often felt like a stray herself, a tattered girl who had lost the comfort of home.

Could she really go back to Oklahoma and see her father? And what about forgiving him? She wasn't sure if her heart was capable.

While Adam packed an overnight bag, Sarah visited with Cameo and the kittens. Groucho peeked over the box at her, his eyebrows quirked at a curious angle. She decided he was contemplating his escape, anxious to develop the skills that would enable him to climb out.

"You're going to be a handful," she told him.

Cameo meowed and sent her a look that said he already was. Sarah grinned and reached for the fluffy little monster. She couldn't wait to take him home. Glancing back at Adam, she cocked her head. He sat at his computer, punching keys.

"What are you doing?"

"Just getting online for a minute."

"What for?"

"To check my e-mail." He studied the screen. "Plus I thought I'd see what kind of airline rates were available. Maybe I can get us a deal." Turning to look over his shoulder, he met her gaze. "You're not going to have any trouble getting time off in August, are you?"

"No." Her schedule was more or less her own. She leased a treatment room from the salon, booking her own hours. "Do you really think we need to get our tickets so soon?"

"Why?" His gaze turned suspicious. "Are you thinking of backing out?"

"No." Yes. Maybe. She wasn't sure. "I've never been on a plane before."

"Really?" The look in his eyes softened. "How did you come to California?"

"On a bus." Which made her feel unsophisticated and poor. Of course that was exactly what she was at the time. A down-and-out Indian with an alcoholic father.

"I can do this tomorrow." He shut down the computer and came toward her, clearly sensing her mood. "Don't change your mind, Sarah. I don't want to go to Oklahoma without you. We both need this."

When he gazed directly into her eyes, she thought about how kind and caring he was. "Okay." She made the vow quietly, her heart fluttering on a wing and a prayer. Somehow she would summon the strength to go home.

Adam stood beside Sarah in her sunny bathroom, shedding his clothes. She turned on the water and adjusted the nozzle to accommodate his height. The shower stall was separate from the tub, barely big enough for one person, let alone two. That made this more stimulating. When he joined her in the confined space, skin brushed skin.

They managed to share the water and the soap. He used her shower gel, lathering his body. She scrubbed, too, washing away the emotion and exhaustion of the day. He could almost see her muscles relax.

She ducked under the spray and saturated her hair. It clung, wet and ropy, to her breasts, like twines of licorice. He imagined putting his mouth there.

He knew he could make love to her, but he wanted to wait. He wanted to fantasize while she touched herself, while she soaped her arms and belly, the V between her legs.

There was nothing more beautiful than a naked woman, especially one who had no idea how exquisite she was.

She washed her hair, and he stood, fully aroused, watching her. Sarah's shampoo smelled sweetly of carnations, the aphrodisiac that had become her signature.

Minutes later, he lathered his own hair with the same shampoo, and even that felt erotic. Her sexual scent was on him now, spicy and fragrant.

She turned, and her nipples grazed his arm. He made a rough sound, but it couldn't be heard above the pounding water. When she looked up at him, trapped him with those dark eyes, he struggled to breathe.

She reached for him, and he knew he was lost.

Sleek and slippery, they rubbed and kissed, like otters

splashing in the sea. He licked moisture from her skin, opened his mouth and let rivulets run onto his tongue.

She brought his head to her breasts. He latched onto a nipple and sucked. Hard. So hard, she clawed his shoulders and moaned.

Soaking wet, they stumbled from the bathroom to her bed, desperate for each other. Sunlight spilled into the room, bathing them in a late-afternoon glow. Still kissing, they shoved the quilt away, finding the sheets cool and inviting.

He wanted to crawl all over her, devour every luscious curve. Taut and erect, he spread her thighs and penetrated her, heat flooding his loins.

He moved, and she moved with him, taking him deeper.

Sex. Sensation. Incredible lovemaking.

It felt different this time. Warmer, wetter, even more intimate.

And then they looked at each other and realized why. They were completely naked, joined with no protection between them.

Adam groaned, then withdrew, even though he ached to stay right where he was.

"Maybe I should get on the Pill," she said.

He stroked her hair. It was still wet and clinging to her skin. "That isn't natural. It isn't good for your body."

She arched against him. "Then what?"

"A holistic method."

She kissed the side of his neck. "They're not foolproof."

"Nothing is." He turned his head and captured her lips. They were discussing birth control, yet they couldn't stop touching. "I wish we could forget about it."

"We can't."

"I know." He knew, but he wanted to lose himself inside her, spill his seed and make a baby. Now. Right now.

The urgency should have stunned him, but it didn't. He was beyond analyzing his feelings. When she was this close, all he could think about was keeping her, holding on and never letting go.

"We need a condom," she reminded him.

"Later." He pushed her down and buried his face between her legs. She gasped on contact, and he tasted her, over and over, delving into warm, wet heat.

Her stomach quivered, her hips bucked. Half crazed, she panted his name and tugged on his damp hair.

Yes, he thought. If he couldn't make a baby, then he wanted it wild.

Slick and sweet and wild.

He reveled in her reaction. Dark-eyed, smooth-skinned Sarah. In that climactic moment, that hot, sexy moment, she belonged to him. Flesh and blood and soul.

She needed him.

When he tore into the condom, they were more than ready. She straddled his lap and impaled herself, riding him until the rest of the world shattered and disappeared.

The sun had yet to rise, but Sarah was awake. She sat up in bed, and Adam stirred beside her.

"What's wrong?" he asked, his voice groggy.

She squinted at the clock. "It's later in Oklahoma." And that meant it was daylight there. "I should call my dad and get it over with."

He turned on the lamp, illuminating the room in a pale glow. "Have you been up all night?"

"More or less." She couldn't lie, not with Adam watching her through concerned eyes. She had lain awake, listening to him breathe. Everything was moving too fast. Her feelings for Adam, her fear of going home. She had made promises, and now she couldn't turn back, no matter how much she wanted to.

Sarah studied her companion. His hair fell loose about his shoulders. He looked sleepy and tousled, a rumpled male wrapped in mauve-colored sheets. Her room wasn't overly feminine, but it was still a little too girlish for a man like Adam.

"I can make some tea," he said. "It might help calm your nerves."

"Okay." Anxious, she watched him climb out of bed.

Sarah felt as if she were tumbling down a hill, her heart sliding straight into her stomach. She eyed the phone and wished she could turn off the light and forget this was happening. She didn't want to talk to her dad, and she didn't want to need Adam so badly, either. But, damn it, here she was, unable to stop the spiral of emotion suddenly consuming her life.

Being alone all these years had been so much easier.

She picked up her father's letters and paged through them again. When Adam re-entered the bedroom, she met his gaze.

"I was looking for his number," she said.

He placed her tea on the dresser. "I'll wait in the living room. I'm sure you would rather do this by yourself."

"No, I wouldn't. Truthfully, I'd like you to stay." She lifted the tea and took a small sip. It contained just the right amount of honey. They had already gotten to know each other's habits. "I'm going to ask my dad about your mom. See if he's heard her name before."

Adam sat on the edge of the bed. "Thank you. I know how difficult this is for you."

"I'll be okay." She dialed the number and listened to the rings. They sounded lonely and faraway. The voice that answered had her gripping the receiver. She recognized her father's graveled tone instantly.

"Hello?"

"Dad, it's me."

"Sarah? I hadn't expected…I can't believe…"

His words drifted, and she envisioned him drinking a cup of strong, black coffee— a brew much more potent than her chamomile tea. Did he have a hangover? Was his skin sallow? His eyes swollen? She wanted to picture him sober but couldn't quite manage it.

"I can't believe you actually called," he said finally, forming a more coherent sentence. When she didn't respond, he asked if everything was all right.

No, she thought, it wasn't. Her heartbeat was racing out of control, her imagination battling scenes from the past.

"Everything's fine."

They talked, but not deeply. Their conversation was strained, both unsure of how to communicate with the other. It became a little easier when she mentioned Adam.

"He's a friend," she said. "And he's looking for his biological mother. He doesn't know much about her. We were hoping you could help."

Sarah's father didn't know anyone named Cynthia Youngwolf, but he promised to question some old acquaintances, ask around the Cherokee community.

When the call ended, she glanced at Adam. He sat quietly, watching her with a gentle expression. It was a look she had come to know well.

"I did it," she said. "I talked to him."

"How did he seem?"

"The same. Different. I don't know. I couldn't tell if he was sober."

"I guess we'll find out soon enough." He skimmed her cheek. "You must be beat. Do you want to try to go back to sleep?"

"I don't think I can."

"Then how about some breakfast?"

Sarah glanced at the window. "It's still dark out."

"I don't mind. Do you?"

"No." She reached for her robe, wondering when she would stop relying on Adam.

Maybe never, she thought, with a flicker of warmth and a twinge of fear. Whatever was happening between them felt right. Scary, but right. Maybe being alone wasn't all that great after all. At least now she was alive, her blood crackling with energy.

They walked into the kitchen together, Sarah wrapped in a terry-cloth robe and Adam half-dressed, his pajama bottoms riding just below his navel. They looked like a couple, she thought, two people who slept in the same bed, shared the same chores.

"Sarah?"

"Yes?"

"What's his name? You've never told me your dad's name."

"William," she said, sensing her life, as well as Adam's, was about to change. But whether those changes were good or bad, she couldn't be sure. She took a deep breath and opened the refrigerator. They would have to go to Oklahoma to find out.

Ten

August was hot, particularly in Oklahoma. But Adam didn't mind. He enjoyed the heat, the land, the place that was part of his history. Sarah sat beside him, quiet one minute, chatty the next. They were headed down a narrow dirt road, passing crooked wood fencing and fascinating old farmhouses.

This was their second day in Oklahoma. Their first had been spent battling jet lag and two delayed flights. By the time they had checked into a motel room in Hatcher, all they cared about was a half-way decent meal and a reasonably comfortable bed.

"Do you think they're okay?" she asked.

He knew she meant the kittens they had left behind. "Sure. Babette will take good care of them." Babette was Adam's landlady, an eccentric old woman who had been a Hollywood starlet in her heyday. She was a little strange, with her thinning bleached hair and fake eyelashes, but he trusted her. She had cats of her own.

Sarah shot him a teasing grin. "Do you know what Babette said about you?"

"What?" he asked, wincing a little. From the expression on Sarah's face, it had to be something embarrassing.

"That she rented to you because you have a great butt."

He kept his eyes on the road and tried not to envision his landlady checking out his backside. "Please tell me you're kidding."

"Sorry. It's the truth. She even asked me about your performance in bed. Wanted to know if you were as good as you looked."

Mortified, he felt his cheeks burn. "I hope to God you didn't answer her."

"Of course I did." Sarah laughed. "I told her you were even better. The poor old woman nearly died on the spot."

Adam shook his head, letting the ridiculous remark go. He figured Sarah was camouflaging her anxiety with humor. The road they traveled led to her father's residence, and he supposed William Cloud waited just as nervously for their arrival.

Following the directions written on a scrap of paper, he turned onto another dirt road. In the distance was a small, rough-hewn house.

"This is it," he said.

Sarah nodded, her breathing audible. She looked suddenly vulnerable, with her flowing black hair and dark, deep-set eyes.

Adam wanted to make this moment easier, but he knew there wasn't anything he could say or do that would change her past. She had to face her father, take control of the hurt and betrayal.

He steered the vehicle toward the graveled driveway. The house appeared old but well kept, the land surrounding it flanked by hills.

It was a simple country setting—a wooden porch, a large bed of grass and scattered trees reaching for the sky. The tiny town of Hatcher was dusty yet charming, a world rife with farmers, ranchers and blue-collar workers.

They knocked on the door, and a medium-built man answered the summons. His graying hair was cut short, his eyes as dark as midnight. He looked as if he had lived a rough life, the lines in his face premature. Adam had no doubt he was William Cloud.

"Dad," Sarah said quietly, making no move toward him.

William lifted his hand to touch her cheek, but dropped it before making contact. "You're all grown-up," he said.

"Yes, well…this is my friend, Adam." She offered an introduction quickly, and the men shook hands.

William's grip was strong and steady, and Adam prayed Sarah's father was as sober as he appeared.

"Come in." The other man stepped back, and Sarah and Adam entered his home. The living room was tidy, with paneled walls painted white and hardwood floors polished to a slick shine. The furniture bore slightly worn cushions and a few scars, but it looked inviting.

"I have pop," William said. "Would you like one?"

Sarah didn't respond, so Adam accepted a soda to be polite. They gathered in the kitchen, around a table with mismatched chairs. It made the old-fashioned room seem sort of art deco, although Adam doubted that had been William's intent. The furniture had probably come from a flea market and had been purchased out of necessity rather than style.

William pointed to a multi-paned window. "See those hills? That's where the rich people around here live. Society types who drive luxury cars. I work at a garage up there." He glanced at his daughter. "They're decent folk, and they treat me right."

Adam assumed that was William's way of saying that he was a respected citizen, a man who had battled the bottle and won. Sarah didn't look impressed or convinced by her father's words, but he understood why. She had been through hell and back with her dad, much in the same way his parents had struggled with him. Trusting an alcoholic wasn't easy.

William turned to Adam. "So you're looking for your biological mother."

"Yes, I am."

"That's good. Family is important." He drew a breath. "I've been doing what I can, asking some old friends if they've ever heard of her. I haven't had any luck, but I'll keep trying."

"Thank you. That means a lot to me. It feels a little strange, being born into a culture I don't know much about."

The older man cocked his head, then chuckled. "As long as you don't tell anyone that your great-grandmother was a Cherokee princess, you'll be fine."

Adam grinned. Sarah had already explained that myth. It seemed just about everyone claiming to have Cherokee blood also claimed they had descended from royalty. But the fact was there were no Cherokee princesses, at least not in the true definition of the word. In years past, Cherokee men had used an endearment for their wives that roughly translated to princess. The royalty fable had become a long-running joke in Indian country.

"Sarah's name means princess in Hebrew," Adam said, smiling at William.

"That's right, it does." The other man quirked an eyebrow. "I guess that means my daughter is a true Cherokee princess."

"Very funny." Sarah looked at her dad, and they both sputtered into nervous laughter.

When their laughter faded, silence engulfed the room. Adam decided it was time to go for a walk. Expressing an interest in the landscape, he rose from the table, leaving father and daughter alone.

He stepped onto the porch, hoping they would take this opportunity to talk.

Sarah sat in silence with her dad, barely meeting his gaze. She didn't know where to begin, what to say, even where to look. Everything in his house had changed. There wasn't one stick of furniture she recognized. Even her father seemed different. Older, she supposed. The lines around his eyes were more pronounced, the shape of his face more angular. His hair hadn't thinned, but it bore an abundance of gray.

How was she supposed to do this? How could she speak her mind when her mind was in a fog? She wanted to hate

William Cloud, to shout at him, but another part of her wanted to lean against him and cry.

"Maybe I should check on Adam," she said, searching for an excuse to escape.

"Why? Is there something wrong with him?"

She twisted the hem on her blouse. "No...I just—"

"He's more than a friend, isn't he?"

Blinking, she stilled her hands, clasping them on her lap. "I don't think that's any of your concern." And she didn't want to admit that she was falling in love, at least not out loud, and certainly not to her wayward father.

"I'm sorry. I didn't mean to upset you. It's just the way you look at him. The way he looks at you." William's voice turned soft. "It was like that with your mother and me. I still miss her."

"I miss her, too."

"She knew I was an alcoholic."

Sarah felt the blood drain from her face. "What are you talking about?"

"I was a drinker when I met her. I've been fighting this practically all of my life."

"And she married you anyway?"

"She loved me."

Sarah's heart lurched, stunned by the frightening pattern, the parallel between herself and her mother.

No, she thought. It wasn't the same. Her situation with Adam was different. He was sober. He wasn't fighting the addiction anymore. "So the whole time you were married to Mom, you were drinking?"

He shook his head. "No. I was on the program. I messed up a few times, but she was there to help me through it."

Betrayal gripped her stomach, twisting it into a painful knot. "And neither one of you ever thought to tell me?"

"I didn't want you to know. Your mother was always talking about the old ways, a man being a warrior and all that. I didn't want to spoil that image for you."

Sarah's eyes burned, but she refused to cry. Lifting her

chin, she swallowed the lump in her throat. "But you did spoil it. After she died, you ruined everything."

"I know. I'm so sorry."

He met her gaze, his dark eyes filled with apology. And something else, she thought. Shame? Sorrow? Loneliness? She couldn't be sure. She had seen the look before, given in to it so many times in the past.

William picked up his soda, drank from the can and placed it back on the table. "I know what it's like to live with an alcoholic. My mother…your grandmother…I don't think she was sober a day of her adult life."

And she had died when Sarah was just a toddler. "You never talked about her. I just assumed that it made you sad, that you missed her."

"My mother was a miserable woman. Bitter. Dirt poor. My father wasn't any better, but he didn't stick around long enough to matter." He glanced out the window. "I was ashamed of where I came from, of who I was."

She followed his gaze to the hills. A part of her understood all too well. "You daydreamed about being rich. And white."

He nodded. "I didn't have any pride in my heritage, not until I met your mother. She was my salvation."

The way Adam is mine, she thought, aware of the irony once again. "Adam's the one who talked me into coming here."

"Are you glad he did?"

"I don't know." Adam had a way of making everything seem all right, but she wasn't sure if it was. "Are you really sober, Dad?"

"Yes. Do you believe me?"

"Not really, no."

"I can't say as I blame you. I've lied before."

"Yes, you have." And she knew how it felt to have him abuse her trust. She couldn't let her heart go, not this time, not so easily. "Why did you move away from Tahlequah?"

"Too many memories," he responded. "And you weren't there anymore. I didn't want to live in that house without you."

"I like California. I've made a life for myself there."

"So you don't miss Tahlequah?"

She missed the way things had been before her mother died, the parental bond, the sense of belonging. "I'm taking Adam there tomorrow."

"I hope he finds his family."

"I hope so, too," she said, turning to look out the window again.

Sarah glanced at Adam, who paged through books at the museum gift shop. They had spent two days in Tahlequah. Yesterday they'd searched for information about his mother and today they'd toured the Cherokee Heritage Center.

She knew the Tsa-La-Gi Ancient Village had fascinated him the most. It was her favorite part of the tour, too. A living museum, the village recreated the lifestyle of the Cherokee during the sixteenth century, a time when being Indian seemed beautiful and romantic. As the "villagers" had gone about their daily routine, Adam and Sarah had envisioned their ancestors preparing food and making arrowheads, weaving baskets and playing stick ball.

Maybe it was okay to feel safe with someone, she thought, to love a man the way she loved Adam. He made Tahlequah seem like a magical place. When she was with him, she didn't dwell on the pain from her past. Even the prospect of seeing her father again wasn't so frightening.

"Look at these." Adam displayed the books in his hand. "Cherokee medicine. Can you believe it? This one is filled with natural plant remedies."

"That's great." Suddenly emotional, she reached for his arm and held tight. "Everything's going to be all right, isn't it?"

"Of course it is." Studying her expression, he kissed her forehead. "We have each other, don't we?"

She breathed in his scent, the herbal soap he used on his skin. "And we're going to find your mom. Maybe not on this trip, but eventually we'll find her." They had to, she thought. Because Adam needed a connection to his roots. He needed to know who he was and where he had come from. Now that she was home, she knew how important that was.

"This means a lot to me," he said. "You being here, helping me look for my mom."

"I know."

He paid for his books, and they headed to a restaurant Sarah recommended. It was a small diner, but the food had a hearty, home-cooked quality. They scooted into a vinyl booth and scanned their menus.

"I've had a good time today," he said.

"Me, too. I wish yesterday had been more productive, though." Their search for Cynthia Youngwolf had led nowhere. No one seemed to remember her, and the tribal office wasn't able to accommodate them. There were over 200,000 enrolled members of the Cherokee Nation. Locating a woman who had given her son up for adoption nearly thirty years before wasn't a simple task.

"How many Youngwolfs are on the final rolls?" she asked, referring to the data Adam had found on the Cherokee enrollment compiled between 1898 and 1914.

"Eleven. But there's no way to link me to any of them."

That was true. The only way for Adam to receive a Certificate of Indian Blood was to provide birth records that proved he was related to someone on the final rolls.

"We should start bright and early tomorrow," Sarah suggested, knowing they couldn't give up hope. " Maybe go to the library first. See if they have any old high-school annuals."

Adam sipped his water. "That's a great idea, but I wish I knew how old she was when I was born. I have no idea when she went to high school."

"We'll just have to cover a couple of decades. And since Youngwolf doesn't appear to be a very common name around here, that should help."

If they found a picture of her in an old yearbook, then they might be able to locate some of her classmates. Someone must have kept in touch with her, Sarah thought. People just didn't fade into oblivion. News about Cynthia would turn up sooner or later.

Adam sat across from Sarah thinking how beautiful she was, how vital she had become to him. He couldn't imagine living without her, but now wasn't the time to tell her how he felt. The diner was noisy and crowded, hardly the right atmosphere for a man to spill his heart.

"We should check out the private schools, too."

He blinked and picked up his fork, pulling himself back into their conversation. "For information about my mom?"

She nodded. "I know of a Christian academy that's been around for quite a while. She could have gone there."

"I hadn't thought of that." And he couldn't begin to express his gratitude. Sarah finally understood how important this was to him.

He cut into his turkey and watched her do the same. They had a lot in common, he thought. They enjoyed the same foods, the same kind of movies. And they were more than compatible in bed. Every time they made love, they clung to each other afterward, as if neither could bear to let go.

He still wanted to make a baby with her, to see her tummy swell with his child. It would be the ultimate connection, a bond that could never be broken.

"Adam?"

"Hmm?"

"What are you thinking about?"

You, he wanted to say. Us. Our future.

"Family," he told her, deciding it was close enough to the truth. "I keep wondering who my dad is and if he still lives around here. He could have gone to high school with my mom. Or he could have been her college sweetheart." And since arriving in Oklahoma, Adam had looked at strangers with interest, realizing they could be his biological parents.

"It's too bad you don't have a copy of your original birth certificate. Your father's name was probably on it."

"Believe me, I tried. I contacted the hospitals in the area, but they couldn't help. I also checked with the Department of Health Services. The records in cases like mine are sealed.

The only birth certificates available are the ones that have been amended.''

"We should still go the hospitals and question the staff. There might be a doctor or a nurse who remembers Cynthia.''

Adam had no idea if he was born in the Tahlequah City Hospital or in the Indian Hospital, but he was willing to talk to whomever would listen. ''You're right. I mean, how many unwed mothers could there have been in those days? Of course, it's been almost thirty years.''

"True, but someone might direct us to a retired employee.''

Lifting his water, he smiled. ''Thanks for helping, Sarah.''

She smiled back at him. ''You're welcome. Do you want to go for a drive after we eat? There's still some historic sites you haven't seen.''

"Sure.'' He glanced out the window and saw the town where he had been born, the streets and sidewalks, the parks and rivers. He had parents out there somewhere. And he had Sarah. He wasn't alone anymore.

"Do you know when abortions were legalized? '' he asked, wondering about the past.

"I'm not sure, but I think the Supreme Court ruling was in 1973.''

"So what were women doing before then?''

"Going to Mexico, I guess.'' She tilted her head, sending him a curious look. ''Why?''

"I'm just glad my mom didn't do that. I'm glad she chose to have me.''

"Me, too.'' Her eyes turned a little misty, but she kept eating, the buzz of the diner swirling around her.

It was a strangely intimate moment, Adam thought. Noisy yet quiet.

Thirty minutes later, they finished their meals, then climbed into the SUV. She drove this time, taking him on a private tour of her hometown. She pointed out sites of interest, historical homes and buildings, the architecture ranging from Victorian to more modern styles.

When they stopped in front of a cemetery, he turned to look at her.

"My mother is buried here," she said. "Do you mind if I visit her grave?"

"Of course not."

She opened her door. "Will you come with me?"

He nodded, then walked across the lawn with her. His adoptive parents were buried in a place just like this one— grass and trees and marble headstones. He knew how it felt to grieve, to kneel on the ground and blink back tears.

Sarah stopped in front of a stone marker, and Adam read the inscription: Nancy Lynn Cloud. Beloved Wife and Mother.

"Someone left flowers." A fresh bouquet spilled onto the grave like a rainbow of love and remembrance.

"It must have been my father." Her voice broke a little, and Adam put his arm around her.

"She knows we're here," he said, certain he could feel Nancy Cloud's spirit.

"Do you think she knows what's happening between us?" Sarah asked.

"Yes." He touched her cheek as she turned to face him. "I'm sure she's watching over us right now."

"It doesn't scare me so much anymore." She looked directly into his eyes, the sun shining on her skin. "I like the feeling."

"So do I." He knew they were talking about love, making a declaration in front of the woman who had given Sarah life. It seemed fitting somehow. "I want to marry you. I want you to have my babies."

She leaned into him, soft and warm and beautiful. "I want that, too."

They didn't talk on the way back to the motel, but he didn't mind. They had already spoken from their hearts. And Sarah had just agreed to become his wife.

The world was a perfect place, he thought, and life couldn't get much better. Love was everything Adam Paige had always hoped it would be.

* * *

The following morning was warm and quiet. Adam breathed against Sarah's hair, and she wondered how long they had slept in this position. Spoon-style, she supposed it was called, his front to her back.

She moved her bottom deliberately, then smiled when he groaned. Apparently he was awake, too. Awake and aroused. She could feel him through the lightweight pajamas he wore.

She turned to face him, to brush his lips. He looked gorgeous, his eyes sleepy, his hair loose and just a little messy. A night-tousled male. Rumpled and sexy.

Was this really happening? Had she really agreed to marry him?

Yes, she thought, tasting his kiss, she had. And she wasn't sorry. She loved him so much, she actually hurt inside.

He nibbled her jaw, and she imagined mornings like this for the rest of her life. And now, she wanted all of him, every powerful muscle, every hard, virile inch.

"Adam?"

"Hmm?"

"How come you've never asked me to—" she paused and toyed with the drawstring on his waistband, "—you know?"

He blinked those sleepy eyes, but she knew he understood the question. Oral sex. An image of the act danced between them like firelight. He did it to her, but she had yet to reciprocate.

"I'd never ask you to do that," he said, his voice shy yet crackling with heat.

It was a stimulating combination. The sound of sandpaper over sun, coarse and warm all at once. In response, she skimmed her hand up and down his belly, making his muscles quiver.

"What if I offered?"

He moistened his lips, then looked at her mouth, studied it with a very quiet, very masculine longing. When he lifted his gaze, they stared at each other. "That's different. I mean, well…"

Sarah couldn't help herself. She had to ask, had to hear him admit it out loud. "So, do you want me to?"

He looked at her mouth again, and her nipples ignited into red-tipped sparks. "Yeah," he said, his sinful voice even raspier. "I do."

With a small, feminine smile, she kissed his chest, moved her hands slowly down his body. And as she tugged on his pajamas, his breath rushed out.

He seemed anxious, maybe even a little nervous, and that thrilled her. She ached to create a new moment between them.

A slick, sensual journey. An erotic awakening.

He was perfect—bronzed and naked and unbelievably hard. His chest narrowed into lean hips, and his legs were long and muscular. A line of hair grew from his navel to his sex. Fascinated, she followed it with her finger.

Adam watched her, knowing his heart pounded much too fast. She was teasing him, making him wait, making him want so badly he could barely breathe. Her lips, warm and tender, cruised over his belly. And then her tongue. So wet, so stimulating.

He was dying. And soon, he thought, soon, he would slide straight into heaven. He fisted the sheets and lifted his hips. Or was it hell? he asked himself, as her hair, that long, luxurious curtain, caressed his thighs. She was an angel, a devil, a vixen who had captured his soul.

Nothing mattered but her.

He was desperate to be touched. Loved. Laved. He chanted her name, over and over in his mind. *Sarah. Sweet, sweet Sarah.* Her mouth was on him now. There, right there.

He struggled to control the urgency, struggled to keep himself from falling too far, but he knew he was losing the battle.

Sensation slammed into sensation, as fast and violent as a storm. His breath crashed in his lungs, his blood pumped heat through his veins

He had to stop her. Now.

Fighting the fury, he gripped her shoulders and pulled her up. Her nightgown was in the way, so he grabbed the fabric and nearly tore it in his haste.

They tumbled over the bed, and he yanked open the drawer and fisted a condom. And then he tried, damn it, tried to tear the package, but he couldn't quite manage it. Sarah was stroking him, milking him with those smooth, skilled hands.

"You shouldn't do that," he rasped. She still wore her panties, and his climax was ebbing, rising like a wave.

"It's okay."

"But I can't...not yet...not..."

"I want you to." She pressed her stomach to his and held him, giving him permission, encouraging him to spill, warm and wet, onto her skin.

And when it happened, he shuddered in her arms and let the moment, the incredible closeness, sweep him away.

Eleven

Three days later, Sarah and Adam sat at the table in their motel room, sharing a makeshift breakfast of fresh fruit and granola bars. They'd showered, but had yet to dress. Both wore terry-cloth robes. Like a happy couple, she thought, lounging on a quiet morning.

Peeling an orange, she glanced up at him. He lifted an apple to his mouth and smiled. Perfect Adam. It was difficult to picture him as a rebellious youth, a teenage boy stealing whiskey and lying to his parents. He was so grounded now, so centered.

"I can't believe we haven't found out anything about your mom," she said.

They had searched, but there was no sign of Cynthia Youngwolf, not one single clue. No one at the hospitals remembered her, nor did the library in town have any old high-school annuals available. The librarian had suggested checking with the schools themselves, but that hadn't panned out, either. Both high schools were closed for the summer.

"We haven't gone to the university yet. She might have been a student there. There's still a lot of ground to cover."

He was right, of course. Their search wasn't over.

Adam took a swig of bottled water. "I'd still like to buy some ranch property around here, Sarah. Are you okay with that?"

Suddenly nervous, she filled her lungs with air, then let it out slowly. "Yes." She wanted to make a life with Adam and that meant coming to terms with her past, with making some kind of peace with her father. "I haven't spent much time with my dad. I should go see him today. I think it's his day off."

"That's a good idea." He reached for her hand, squeezed it. "Everything's going to be fine, sweetheart."

"I know," she said, even though she felt a niggle of fear. But with Sarah, there were always little jabs of worry. It was her nature, she supposed.

Abandoning breakfast, Adam shed his robe. "We can meet here later."

"Are you going to the university?"

"No. I'd rather wait for you to do that."

"Then what are you going to do?"

He grinned. "Go see a Realtor. They've already got a list of properties to show me."

"We only have one car," she pointed out.

"I can walk. The realty office isn't far from here."

Adam was dressed before Sarah, but it was easier for a man to throw himself together. All he needed was pair of jeans and a T-shirt to look gorgeous. Her ritual consisted of quite a bit more.

He buckled his belt and reached for his shoes. "There's a nice seafood restaurant down the street. How about some swordfish tonight?"

"Sure." She curled a mascara wand around an eyelash, doing her best to prevent it from clumping.

"Feel free to invite your dad."

"Okay."

After lacing his ropers, he patted her bottom. She laughed

and nearly poked herself in the eye. "You better get out of here before I end up with an injury."

"Yes, ma'am." He faked an Oklahoma twang. "I'll see you back here around five."

She watched him go, feeling like a schoolgirl. Her heart was fluttering in her chest. Just like the patter of little feet, she thought. Someday she was going to have his babies.

And there was nothing to worry about, she told herself as she dialed her father's number. This wasn't a dream. She wasn't going to wake up and find everything gone. They had already picked out names for their children. And Adam was meeting with a Realtor, looking for a home.

What could be more stable than that?

Her dad's line was busy, so she went back to her makeup. When she called again, he answered.

"Hi," she said. "It's me. I was wondering—"

"Oh, God. I was just going to call you."

Her fluttering heart skipped a beat. "Why? What's going on?"

"Nothing. I mean, I don't want to talk about it over the phone."

He's been drinking, she thought. His voice sounded shaky, his words unsteady. How could he do this? And what excuse would he come up with to ease his conscience?

"Can you come over, Sarah?"

She wanted to say no. She wanted to tell him to go straight to hell. "Yes," she said instead.

"Will you come alone? I don't want Adam—"

"He isn't here." But she wished he was. She didn't know how she was going to handle this without him.

The drive to Hatcher took forever. The roads to her father's house were long and dusty, and in spite of the air-conditioned vehicle, her palms were sweating.

He met her on the porch, reaching out to take one of her clammy hands.

He looked distressed. And with her father, that meant a shot or two. Or three, she thought, releasing a pent-up breath. "How many have you had, Dad?"

"What?" He backed away, releasing her hand. "Is that what you think this is about?"

She crossed her arms. The sun was beating down on her back. She had prepared herself for the heat, worn a sleeveless shirt and fastened her hair in a single braid, but the humidity stuck to her like glue. "Isn't it?"

"No. This has nothing to do with me. It concerns Adam."

Skeptical, she tilted her head. "Really? How so?"

"I found out about his mother, honey. And his father, too."

Her knees nearly buckled. "I'm sorry. I thought—"

"It's okay. Come inside and we'll talk."

She sat on her dad's old-fashioned sofa and waited for him to sit beside her. But instead, he paced the floor, then stopped to drag a hand through his hair. It must be bad, she thought. Really bad.

"Are they dead?" she asked.

William frowned. "His father is."

"And his mother?"

"She's in Tulsa."

Then it can't be that bad, Sarah told herself. As long as Cynthia Youngwolf was alive, there was hope. "Is she sick?"

"No." He sat beside her, sinking into the corduroy cushions. "She's a widow and has other children. Two grown sons and a school-age daughter."

Sarah's heart stuck in her throat. Adam had brothers. And a little sister. She tried to picture them, wondered if they were as beautiful, as perfect as the man she loved. "They don't know about him, do they?"

"No, they don't." He stared straight ahead. "I'm sorry, honey, but Adam's mother doesn't want to see him."

"Why?" Anger caught her hard and fast. She didn't have any sympathy for Cynthia Youngwolf, not if the woman was going to hurt Adam. There had been a time when Sarah thought he had been wrong to search for his family, but she felt differently now. "This isn't fair. All he wants is a chance to meet her. He deserves that much."

"Honey, you don't understand."

She narrowed her eyes. "Then make me understand. Tell me why she doesn't want to see her son."

"I will," he said. "But how in God's name we're supposed to tell Adam, I don't know."

When Adam walked into the motel room, he shot Sarah and William a big smile, pleased that her father had decided to join them. "So we're on for dinner?" He couldn't wait to tell them about the properties he had seen.

"We need to talk." Sarah, sitting on the edge of the bed, looked up at him. She seemed sad, he realized suddenly. He glanced at William, who stood near his daughter. His expression was equally somber.

"What's going on?"

"I found your mother." William stepped forward. "And I'm going to start from the beginning, because I don't know how else to do this."

Adam sat in a chair by the desk. In that instant, he knew: Cynthia Youngwolf had refused to meet him. All of Sarah's old warnings came scrambling back, tenfold.

I hate to say this, but there's a good chance that your biological mother won't want to see you. She might feel as though you're interfering in her life.

Preparing himself for the worst, he maintained his composure. He would listen to whatever William had to say, and when it ended, he would give his mother the time she needed. Eventually, it would work out.

When William's breath hitched, he wanted to tell the other man that everything would be okay. He understood how difficult this had to be for his mother. She wasn't expecting to hear from him. It had to be a shock.

"You weren't born in a hospital," William told him. "A midwife delivered you. Her name is Margaret, and she's the one who told me about your mother. Margaret is an old woman now, but she never forgot Cindy Youngwolf."

"Cindy? Is that the name my mom uses?"

He nodded. "Yes."

"Whose house was I born at?"

"Cindy's aunt's. You see, your mother wasn't from Tahlequah. She lived in Oklahoma City at the time, but she had an aunt here. So when her family found out she was pregnant, they sent her to stay with a relative."

"How old was Cindy?" he asked, trying to picture his mother.

"Eighteen. She was a quiet girl who kept to herself, but she told Margaret about what had happened to her."

He sat forward in his chair. "What do you mean?"

"I wish I didn't have to tell you this."

Sarah glanced away, and Adam's stomach fell. Why wouldn't she look at him? And why was her father so reluctant to talk? What the hell was going on? "Just say it."

William bit down on his bottom lip. "Cindy claimed that she was raped. That a white boy had forced her to…" The older man glanced up at the ceiling. "But in those days, if a girl flirted with a boy, she was held accountable, too. The police discouraged her from filing charges. She was a minority, and he came from a well-to-do family. That's the way things were back then."

"No." Adam shook his head. "The midwife has my mother mixed up with someone else." This sordid, sickening story didn't belong to him. "My mother and my father were—" in love, he wanted to say. His eyes stung, but he fought the urge to cry. "They…" When his voice broke, he looked at Sarah and saw that her hands were trembling. "Oh, God. Who are they, William? Who the hell are my parents?"

"Cindy Youngwolf is your mother. And your father was a twenty-year-old college boy."

"I don't want to be related to him. I don't…"

"I'm sorry."

Adam battled a wave of nausea. His mother, his eighteen-year-old mother, was sexually assaulted. By his father. His conception was a vile act, the most degrading of human crimes. "How could he do that to her? How could he…" The nausea worsened, so he stood and made his way to the sink. He wanted to vomit, but he knew it wouldn't help. He couldn't purge his father's sin.

Turning, he faced William again, feeling shamed and dirty. "Who is he?"

"A college boy," the other man said again, his voice filled with sorrow.

"What's his name? What's the bastard's bloody name?"

"I don't know. If it's any consolation, he's dead. Margaret said that he's been dead a long time."

"Good." It didn't help, not really, but he unclenched his fists. If his father wasn't dead, he would have called him out, taken vengeance for Cindy. And for the disgusting circumstances of his birth.

When Sarah started toward him, he backed himself against the sink. She was crying, blinking furiously to stop the flow. Who did she see? he wondered. Who was he to her now?

"Don't touch me." He held up his hand to ward her off. She was too pure to come into contact with him, too soft and beautiful. His blood was tainted. He could feel it running through his veins like a sewer of filth.

He hadn't been prepared for this, for something so dirty. And by searching for Cindy, by showing up nearly thirty years later, he had brought the memory back to her, the ache and the horror of being violated.

"Do you think my mother tried to wash him off her skin?" he asked, his mind clouding with heart-wrenching images. "Do you think she rubbed her body until it was raw?" Because no one answered, he continued to talk. "That's what I've heard women do after they're raped. They try to make themselves clean again."

"You have to stop thinking about that," William said. "Your mother went on with her life. She got married, and she had other children. She's widowed now, but her daughter is only twelve. And her sons are close by."

A lump clogged Adam's throat. Cindy had given birth to other babies, children she wanted. He tried to be glad for her, but all he felt was pain. He was the one she had given away, the baby who had grown in her stomach like a cancer.

He was the rape.

"I want you to go home," he told William. "And I want you to take Sarah with you."

"No." She was still crying, her hands still trembling. "I love you, Adam. Let me stay with you."

He closed his eyes. He needed to send Sarah as far away as he could. She pitied him now, but before long, her skin would start to crawl. She would look at him and see the cancer. He was no longer the man she loved. He couldn't give her sweet, clean babies. His genes were soiled.

How could she stand to look at him? Even think about touching him?

"Please." Opening his eyes, he implored the other man. "I need some time alone."

William took charge, insisting his daughter pack an overnight bag. She gathered a few toiletries and whispered a shaky goodbye.

Adam turned away and waited for them to leave, and when they were gone, he caught his reflection in the mirror.

Without thinking, he raised his fist to the glass and shattered it. Blood dripped down his wrist, but he didn't care. It was his father's face that he had just destroyed, and he never wanted to see it again.

At dawn, Sarah stared at the flickering image on the television set. She had covered herself with a blanket, but felt no warmth from it. All she could think about was Adam.

A shadow crossed the room, and she turned to see her father.

His hair was wet from a recent shower, the salt and pepper strands combed away from his face. "You haven't slept, have you?"

She shook her head. "What are you doing up so early?"

"Getting ready for work." He sat beside her and handed her a cup. "I don't have any tea, but I thought you might need this."

"Thanks." Accepting the offering, she brought it to her lips. It was coffee, diluted with cream and sugar. She let the liquid seep into her bones, chasing away the chill.

"It's morning now," he said. "It would probably be okay to go see him."

"That's what I was thinking." She turned to look out the window, where the sun peeked through the blinds, sending slats of light across the hardwood floor. It could have been a rainbow, but she knew better. "Is he going to be all right?"

"Of course, he is. He has you, doesn't he? You'll help him get through this."

"Just the way I have you." She smiled at her father, remembering how she had cried in his arms the night before. "Are my eyes still puffy?"

"Yeah, but it doesn't make you any less pretty."

"I love you, Dad."

"I love you, too." He squeezed her knee. "Now go on, get yourself together. There's a man who needs you more than I do."

She stood and sipped her coffee. And at that moment, in the light of dawn, with cartoons playing on TV and the taste of caffeine on her tongue, she knew William Cloud was sober.

He winked at her, and she saw her daddy—the strong, proud warrior who used to tuck her in at night. Before she broke down and started crying again, she headed for the shower, reviving herself for Adam.

An hour later, Sarah unlocked the motel-room door. The bed was still made, the curtains drawn tight, keeping out the light. She stepped farther into the darkness, willing her eyes to adjust. Placing her purse on the desk, she turned, her heart catching on a gasp.

"Oh, dear God."

He was asleep on the floor, his bloodied hand staining his shirt. The mirror above the sink was smashed. Shards of glass littered the counter, glinting dangerously.

She knelt on the carpet and touched his shoulder. He flinched and came awake, jerking when he saw her.

"Shhh. It's okay. I'm just going to clean up your hand."

He didn't protest, so she wet several washcloths in the tub and sat on the floor in front of him. There were slivers of glass under his skin and gashes deep enough to worry her.

"You might need stitches."

He pulled back. "It doesn't matter."

It did to her, but she didn't press the issue. Tending him the best she could, she removed the glass with a pair of tweezers and cut the corner of a sheet for a makeshift bandage.

He didn't look like himself. His eyes were empty, so vacant she feared he had lost his soul. Beautiful Adam, she thought, blinking back tears. Her dragon slayer was dying inside, slipping into a dungeon of darkness and pain.

"It will get easier," she told him, bandaging his hand. She considered drawing him into her arms, but sensed he wouldn't welcome her sympathy. His shoulders were broad and rigid, a man keeping himself at bay. "You won't feel this way forever."

He met her gaze without really looking at her. "I don't care."

But he did, she thought. He cared too much. He wanted his mother to forgive him for something he had nothing to do with. "You were a baby. It wasn't your fault."

"She's ashamed of me. I'll always be something vile in her mind."

"She doesn't even know you. If she did, she would be proud of the man you've become."

He drew his knees up, putting a shield between them. "She should have had an abortion. She should have ended it a long time ago."

"No." Sarah shook her head, wanting to shake him. "Don't you say that. Don't you dare." Because it meant that he didn't think he was worthy of life. And he was. If anyone deserved to be happy, to be loved, it was Adam.

"I'm so stupid." He wrapped his arms around his legs, putting pressure on his hand. Blood seeped through the bandage, staining a portion of the white cloth a crimson hue. "I fantasized about my parents. About how in love they must have been."

"Your other parents were in love. The ones who raised you, Adam. They were your *real* parents."

He looked up, fear in his eyes. "Oh, God. They knew, didn't they? They must have known."

"It doesn't matter—"

"The hell it doesn't." The fear turned to fury, flashes of fire and anger. "All those years, all that time, they knew. When I became a problem, they must have worried that they'd made a mistake, that they'd adopted the wrong child."

"Stop it! They loved you. Don't degrade their memory like this."

"So what am I supposed to do? Pretend that my father didn't rape my mother? Pretend that Cindy isn't refusing to see me? Am I just supposed to go on with my life, feeling normal?"

Sarah couldn't swallow her shame. Adam's world had just shattered. Everything he cared about had been stolen from him, and she didn't have the words to comfort him. Suddenly loving him wasn't enough. "I'm sorry. I wish I could take the pain away."

"You can't. No one can."

Cindy Youngwolf could, she thought. The older woman could meet her son. She could look into his eyes and help him feel human again. But how was that going to happen? Adam's mother didn't want to have anything to do with him.

He came to his feet, and she could see how dizzy he was. He leaned against the wall for support, then steadied himself, rigid once again.

"I need to clean up this mess," he said. "And I have to tell someone at the front desk that I'll have the mirror fixed."

So proper, she thought, so decent. He might be battling a deep state of depression, but he was still concerned about doing the right thing.

"I'll help." She reached for the trash can and began filling it with broken glass. His blood had dried on the counter, and the sight of it made her eyes water. "What are you going to do about your hand?"

Focusing on their task, he shrugged.

"You should see a doctor." She wet a cloth and wiped the counter. "Will you do that, Adam? Will you see a doctor?"

"I guess." He turned to look at her. "Thank you, sweet Sarah, but you should go. You shouldn't be here."

Sweet Sarah. The nickname shot through her like an arrow, piercing the part of her that ached for him. "Come to my father's house with me. It's quiet there." And maybe, just maybe, being in the country would help him heal. "It was so pretty this morning. The sun rises over the hills, and the air smells like horses and hay and flowers. And my dad's neighbor has kids. A boy and a girl. They're part Indian. Like you."

"I'm not part anything anymore." He touched her cheek with his injured hand, brushing her skin with the bandage. "But you…you're so beautiful. Your blood is so pure."

"My blood is no different than yours."

"It's pure," he said again. "Pure Cherokee. I'm what society used to call a half-breed. I don't belong to either side."

She understood what he meant, and because she did, she didn't know how to respond. His mother wouldn't acknowledge him, and his father wasn't worth being related to. It was so unfair. He deserved better. So much more.

He dropped his hand. "Go home. Go back to your dad's, and I'll see a doctor. I'm not going to hurt myself again."

But he wanted to, she thought with despair. He wanted to.

Adam returned from the doctor's office, his hand stitched and bandaged. He'd rented another car so he could distance himself from Sarah. He needed to be alone, to deal with his feelings in his own way. He couldn't share anything with her, not even something as simple as a rental vehicle.

Squaring his shoulders, he entered the motel lobby, intending to get this over with as quickly as possible. He wasn't in the mood to chat with strangers, to fake a smile or return a casual hello.

The lobby was fairly busy. The clerk waited on an older man, and a young couple with a trio of active kids gathered brochures and planned their day.

To keep himself from making direct eye contact with anyone, Adam studied the floor, hoping he appeared as unapproachable as he felt.

When the room finally cleared, he walked toward the desk.

"Hey. How ya doin'?" the clerk said, recognition in his upbeat tone, an indication that he recalled checking Adam and Sarah into their room.

Suddenly Adam didn't know how to explain the situation. Keeping his bandaged hand below the counter, he frowned. He'd told the doctor he'd cut himself on some glass, but this was different. He'd damaged property. This wasn't about his injury.

"I broke the mirror in my room," he said, keeping it honest and simple. "I apologize, and I'm more than willing to replace it."

The clerk measured him with a curious stare, and Adam caught his own blunder. He shouldn't have come in here with a dark cloud hovering over his head, with a don't-mess-with-me stance. He should have called, handled it over the phone.

"Is everything all right?" the other man asked.

"Yeah. It was an accident. You can bill my credit card to fix it."

"And that little lady you're with is all right, too?"

Stunned and immediately sickened, Adam felt his stomach roll. Did the clerk think he had hurt Sarah? Was that the sort of person he appeared to be? A man who abused women? A man like the bastard who had spawned him?

"She's fine."

"So long as she didn't cut herself, too. I noticed your bandage when you came in."

Adam blinked, realizing he'd misunderstood the clerk's concern for Sarah. Was this how he'd react for the rest of his life? Guilty and paranoid about his father's sin? "My hand isn't as bad as it looks."

"Well, then." The other man's posture relaxed. "Why don't I get you checked into another room while we get that one squared away?"

"Thank you."

Five minutes later, Adam exited the lobby, his breath clogging his lungs. He returned to the old room and packed his belongings along with what Sarah had left behind.

And when he entered the new room, he panicked. What was he supposed to do? Stare blindly at the TV? Pace the floor like a caged animal? Struggle to block the fear? The paranoia?

Damn it. The walls were closing in.

He needed to go for a drive. He needed…

His next thought hit him like a fist. A drink. He needed a drink.

No, he told himself as he headed toward his car. No. He was clean, sober. He'd followed a holistic path, healing his mind, respecting his body.

Adam dug the key out of his pocket and ran his thumb over the serrated edge. Big deal. Big damn deal. His adoptive parents were dead, his father was a monster, and his mother couldn't bear to see his face. How holistic was that?

He unlocked the door, slid behind the wheel. And then there was Sarah, he thought. Sweet, sweet Sarah. She had been right from the beginning. They should never have gotten involved, never made love, never fooled themselves into believing everything would be okay. She was too good for him, too wholesome and pure. And if they stayed together, he'd only end up ruining her life.

Like a man possessed, a man losing his soul to an old, familiar demon, he pulled out of the parking lot.

He would buy a bottle of whiskey and go back to his room. And when it was over, when the amber liquid warmed his gut and the edges of his nightmare turned a misty shade of gray, eleven years of sobriety wouldn't mean a thing.

Twelve

————

That evening, Sarah sat on her father's porch, watching the sun set. The sky was a haze of mauve, streaked with slashes of red and melting streams of blue. It reminded her of fire, of flames burning in the heavens. And in her heart.

If only she could make things right for Adam. She had been trying to reach him for hours, leaving messages at the motel. The man at the front desk had told her he'd switched rooms, which made her feel a little better. At least he wasn't staring into the remnants of that broken mirror.

Should she drive over there? Or would that upset him even more? He seemed determined to keep her at bay, to handle this crisis on his own. She suspected he was sitting alone in the dark, refusing to answer the phone.

William came outside and set a plate on the table positioned beside her. "It's that wild rice medley your mom used to make." He pointed to the dinner he'd prepared. "It was your favorite when you were little. You never cared much for burgers and fries and that sort of thing. You always went for the healthier stuff. It was hard to believe you were my kid. I thrived on junk.''

She picked up the plate and managed a grateful smile. He'd added zucchini from his neighbor's garden to the recipe, and there was a heap of coleslaw and diced apples on the side. "This is perfect. Aren't you having any?"

He wrinkled his nose. "No way. I made myself a sloppy Joe. I'll be right back."

He returned with his meal, and when he bit into the sandwich, bits of the stuffing fell out the sides and landed back on his plate in a saucy mess. He'd given himself potato chips as a side dish and a can of grape soda to wash it down. Sarah sipped bottled water and marveled at the man William Cloud had become.

"I know you're not drinking any more, Dad. And I'm proud of you."

"Thanks." He wiped his mouth. "It's been a long, dark road, and I don't have any intention of going back."

"I should have stayed here. I should have been more supportive, the way Mom was."

"No. You did the right thing. You were young, with your whole life ahead of you. I had no right to put you through that kind of misery, to make you ashamed of me and your heritage." He went after a handful of chips, his actions more casual than his words. "Now I go to a meeting every day. Sometimes twice a day when temptation rears its ugly head."

"You've come a long way." And it made her glad that he was her father, that he was the man her mother had fallen in love with.

"Adam used to drink," she admitted, knowing it was time to confide in her dad. "But he's been sober for eleven years."

William startled, his soda teetering for a moment. "I'm surprised you got involved with him."

"I almost didn't. But I've learned to trust him."

Silence bounced between them then, the sky still blazing with fiery hues. The fragrance of summer misted the air, and Sarah breathed in the scent.

"I love him so much, Dad."

"I know." Balancing his plate on his lap, William frowned into his food. "But are you sure he won't drink again? He is going through a rough time."

As an image of Adam sleeping on the floor loomed in her mind, she shivered. Broken glass and blood. That's how he felt, she realized. Shattered and wounded.

But that didn't mean he would turn to alcohol, she told herself, as a stab of fear jabbed her chest. Adam knew better. He was stronger than that. "I used to think the trigger was out there somewhere, that he might fall, but he said it would never happen."

"And you believe him?"

She nodded. Loving him meant that she had to believe him, had to trust his words, his promises. "Everyone who used to drink doesn't falter." And Adam deserved her support, her faith in his sobriety. "Eleven years is a long time."

"I'm sorry. I had to ask." William released a heavy breath. "Maybe we can convince him to stay here. He should be around family."

"I already tried." Sarah looked up at the sky, suddenly aware of what she had to do. Family was exactly what Adam needed. "Did you talk to Cindy Youngwolf?"

"No. Margaret is the one who called her and told her about Adam. And then she relayed their conversation back to me."

"But you have Cindy's number?"

"Yes. It's listed in the book, under her husband's name. Why? What are you going to do?"

"I'm going to call her," she said, praying the other woman would take the time to listen.

Adam stared at the bottle, at the whiskey he'd purchased hours ago. He hadn't broken the seal, hadn't opened it.

It sat on the dresser like a cool, dark temptation. He wanted it so badly, yet he couldn't bring himself to take that first drink.

Because of Sarah. Because he'd promised her he would never deceive her again. And drinking behind her back would have been the biggest deception of all.

He glanced at the phone. How many messages had she left? Three? Four?

He had to call her, he realized. He had to tell her the truth.

Adam dialed her father's number, keeping his back to the mirror. He'd been avoiding his reflection all night, avoiding the image that sickened him.

"Hello?" Sarah's voice came over the phone, soft and sweet and gentle.

"Hi. It's me." The guy losing his self-respect, the liar, the cheat. He reached for the bottle, felt the familiar shape beneath his fingers. "I'm sorry I didn't call you back sooner."

"Oh, Adam. I have so much to tell you. Can I come by?"

"It's late, Sarah. I don't want you driving over here." And he didn't want her in this room, in the place where he battled the urge to get sloppily drunk. "I rented a car today. I'll head over that way, okay?" So he could tell her in person, look into her eyes and admit what he'd almost done.

"Okay. I love you," she said.

A lump formed in his throat. He loved her, too. More than he had a right to. "I'll be there as soon as I can."

Feeling clumsy and awkward, Adam laced his boots, then cursed his injured hand. And when he stood, he noticed the trembling.

Was he nervous? he asked himself. Or was he experiencing a psychological withdrawal? A mental reminder of the shakes, the edginess that came with the addiction?

Being seventeen years old and craving one shot, just one stress-relieving drink, wasn't something he was likely to forget. Nor was shivering until his teeth rattled.

Adam grabbed the rest of Sarah's luggage and put it in the trunk, along with the whiskey, the proof he needed to set her free, to convince her that loving him was a mistake.

When he arrived at her father's house, she waited for him on the front steps, looking like a little girl in an oversized T-shirt and baggy jeans. She'd plaited her hair into a single braid, leaving the angles of her face unframed. Her eyes seemed darker and deeper, he thought. Her cheekbones more striking. The backlight from the porch bathed her in a soft, buttery glow.

He moved to the back of the car, prepared to open the trunk, to show her the bottle. He couldn't drag this moment out, make either one of them suffer longer than necessary.

She stood and came toward him. "I'm so glad you're here. I talked to your mother, Adam. I talked to Cindy."

He froze, the trunk key imprinting his thumb. "What?"

"I called her." She drew a breath, gauged his troubled expression. "Please don't be mad. I wasn't trying to interfere."

"I'm not mad." He was stunned. Guilty. Sick at heart. He'd spent the day lusting after a drink, and Sarah had contacted his mother. "What did she say?"

"Truthfully, not much. She didn't want to discuss anything personal over the phone. I think her daughter was there."

He closed his eyes, and then opened them a second later. He wouldn't let his mind conjure an image of his mother's youngest child. His little sister.

Sarah moved closer. "Cindy agreed to meet with me tomorrow." She lifted her eyes to his, held him tenderly within her gaze. "And I'm going to tell her about you. About how kind and decent you are."

God help him, he thought. He longed to touch Sarah's cheek, to stroke her skin and profess how much he loved her. But her good intentions didn't change who or what he really was—an alcoholic conceived from rape. "Don't glorify me to my mother. I bought a bottle of whiskey today, right after I switched rooms."

Dear God. Fear, shock, a dizzying pain gripped Sarah's heart. Her father had warned her, but she hadn't seen it coming. Her love for Adam had blinded her, the fairy tale, the fantasy she had created in her mind.

Needing to sit, to collect her emotions, she found her way to the steps. She couldn't fall apart. Not now.

"Did you drink?" she asked.

"No." He shook his head. "I wanted to, though. A lot."

But he didn't, she thought, as her heartbeat stabilized. He

hadn't let himself go that far. He was still living by the vow he'd made to stay sober. The warrior in Adam was fighting the addiction. "You're going to be all right. You'll get through this. I can help you."

"How?" He turned, paced a little, stopped to look at her. "You can't make the craving go away. You're not me, Sarah. You don't know what it feels like. How badly I wanted to open that bottle."

She inhaled the summer air, telling herself to think, to say the right thing. All those years with her father hadn't prepared her for this moment. She wasn't supposed to have fallen in love with an alcoholic. Yet Adam, troubled Adam, lived inside her.

She glanced up at the sky, saw a scatter of stars twinkling against the night. Was there anything she could say or do that would lessen his fears? He seemed so lost, so broken. "You should get professional help. My father goes to meetings. You could—"

"No." He cut her off. "I'm not...I can't..."

He paced again, trampling grass beneath his shoes. His hair was loose, flowing to his shoulders, and his eyes were dark and shadowed. She could see that he hadn't slept, hadn't eaten. She wanted to reach out and hold him, but she knew she couldn't coddle his addiction.

"Why won't you see someone, Adam? You've done it before. You know therapy can be effective."

He dragged a hand through his hair. "It's different this time."

"Why?"

"It just is."

Because of his parents, she realized. His biological parents. Therapy would mean talking about them, admitting out loud why he had the urge to drink. His father had raped his mother, and now his mother was rejecting him.

Sarah thought about Cindy. The other woman hadn't made any promises on the phone. She hadn't agreed to meet Adam, but she had made arrangements to talk to Sarah, to discuss the son she'd given up. It was a start, a hope to cling to. If

Sarah could convince Cindy to give Adam a chance, then maybe he could find the strength to heal.

She looked up at him, saw that he watched her. "Are you hungry?" she asked. "I can heat some leftovers."

"Thanks, but no. I can't deal with food right now. Maybe I just need to get some sleep."

"You can stay here," she offered.

"No. I can't." He came forward and sat beside her. "You promised yourself you'd never get involved with an alcoholic, and that's what I am. A man craving a drink."

Sarah forced herself to breathe, to fill her lungs with oxygen. She wouldn't lose him, not like this. Not to an addiction, to a bottle of whiskey. He was worth so much more than that. "I'm not giving up on you. Or on us."

He touched her cheek, then drew back quickly, his injured hand shaky. "So you're still going to meet with my mother? Tell her what a great guy I am?"

"Yes, I am. And I'm going to be here if you need me." She noticed the professional bandage on his hand, pleased that he'd seen a doctor. "But I'm asking you to destroy the whiskey you bought. Throw it away. Pour it down the sink. Whatever you have to do to get rid of it."

"What if I give it to you?"

She blinked. "What?"

He gestured toward the car. "It's in the trunk. I brought it with me. And I brought the rest of your luggage, too. The stuff you left at the motel."

She ignored the pain, the clench in her heart. Adam couldn't bear to have her staying with him. He had chosen solitude over love.

He placed her suitcase on the porch. And when he handed her the unopened whiskey, she fought a burst of panic, realizing how close to the edge he really was.

Stay strong, she told herself an instant later. Focused. Adam's mother was most likely the key to his salvation.

But would Cindy Youngwolf listen to what Sarah had to say? Would the other woman agree to meet her son? Or would Sarah have to give Adam more hurtful news?

She glanced at the whiskey and frowned. Maybe she was placing too much importance on Adam's mother. Cindy could ease the part of him that ached, but she couldn't stop him from drinking. Only Adam could conquer his addiction.

"I'll call you tomorrow," she said. "After I see your mom."

"Thank you." He looked directly into her eyes. "Aren't you worried that I'm going to buy another bottle?"

"I trust you," she told him. Maybe even more than he trusted himself. Because if she gave into the panic and lost hope, then he would, too.

The following afternoon Sarah drove to Tulsa. She found the park Cindy Youngwolf-Nichols had directed her to and got out of the car.

Anxious, she sat on a picnic bench and placed two small cartons of orange juice on the table. The air was warm, even in the shade. Checking the time, she turned to watch the activity on the playground. A group of kids took turns on the slide, and a toddler clapped his chubby hands and grinned as his mother pushed him on one of the baby swings.

Did Cindy live nearby? Was this the park she had taken her own children to? Or was this on the other side of town, away from those who knew her? Cindy's address wasn't listed in the phone book.

Within minutes a woman came toward the bench. Sarah assumed she was Adam's mother simply because she wore a yellow blouse—the color Cindy had said she would be sporting.

Nervous, she stood to greet her. "Hello," she said, when they were close enough to hear each other. "I'm Sarah."

"Hello." The other woman stood a little awkwardly. Attractive for her age, she was trim, with dark hair cut into one of those easy-to-care-for styles that fell just below her chin. Neither tall nor short, her height measured somewhere in-between.

Because Sarah searched for a family resemblance, she found several. Brown eyes, Indian cheekbones and a mouth that managed to look full and feminine on Cindy, yet wickedly sensual on Adam. Yes, she thought, this woman was his mother.

"I brought some juice."

"Thank you." They both sat, and Cindy accepted one of the plastic containers without opening it. "So Adam is your fiancé?" she asked, reaffirming what had been briefly discussed over the phone.

"Yes, but he's pulling away from me." Trying to convince her not to love him, she thought. And refusing to get help for his struggle, for the battle to stay sober.

"I'm sorry if he isn't taking this well, but this hasn't been easy on me, either. My other children don't know about him. I never even told my husband. I agreed to meet with you because—" Pausing to twist the gold band on her left hand, she trapped Sarah's gaze. "I need for you to understand why I can't see Adam. Why it would be better to leave things as they are."

"That's fine." She would let Cindy say her piece, then she would say hers. She wasn't going to argue with Adam's mother, but she couldn't bear to watch the man she loved suffer, either.

"Giving up a child was the hardest thing I've ever done, but I did it for the right reasons. I wanted him to have a better life than I was able to provide."

"And that's the only reason you didn't keep him?"

"No." The other's woman's gaze turned candid. "It was also because of what his father did to me."

Silent, Sarah waited, knowing she was about to hear the whole ugly story.

Clasping her hands, Cindy placed them on the table. "He was very handsome. Johnny, that was his name. Tall and broad, with the most stunning smile I had ever seen."

"Where did you meet him?"

"At the diner where I worked. Some of the local college students hung out there, so it was an exciting job for me. I was a senior in high school, trying to look more grown-up. I flirted with Johnny, but so did other girls. He got a lot of attention. And he had a wild streak, a rebelliousness that fit the times. We were the generation that was going to change the world.''

Sarah glanced at the playground again. Laughter drifted through the air, as warm and happy as sunshine. No one would ever know, she thought, that two women were sitting below a bright blue sky, discussing the man who had raped one of them.

''One night, after my shift, Johnny asked me to go for a drive. I barely knew him, aside from the little bit of flirting that we'd done, but I wasn't about to refuse. He seemed so nice, so charming.'' Lifting her hand, she smoothed her hair, even though there wasn't a strand out of place. ''And when he took me into a secluded area, I thought 'Oh, my. He's going to kiss me.' He did, of course. But then everything changed. He started tugging at my clothes, pushing me onto the back seat. I said no, and suddenly he wasn't Johnny anymore. He wasn't the charming boy with the stunning smile.''

''I'm so sorry.'' Sarah could almost picture herself in Cindy's place. Naive and young, being abused by someone she had trusted.

''When he was done, I was in tears, and he kept telling me to quit making such a big deal about it.'' She drew a tight breath. ''Later I discovered that my thighs were bruised. And I had a bump on the back of my head because he'd shoved me against the window.''

''Did you tell anyone that night?''

''No. I should have, but I was too ashamed. My parents were asleep, so I crept into the house, took a scalding bath and cried like a baby. When I finally got the courage to tell my mother, the bruises were gone.''

''It was too late then,'' Sarah found herself saying.

''Yes, it was. The police said it would be my word against his. One of them even asked me why I was out to ruin Johnny's life. He was just a college kid, and he came from a good, upstanding family.'' Anger flashing in her eyes, she shook her head. ''Needless to say, my parents convinced me to drop the charges. We were supposed to forget that it ever happened.''

But they couldn't forget, Sarah thought. Not when Cindy turned up pregnant. ''They sent you to Tahlequah to have your baby.''

She nodded. ''And while I was gone, they moved from Oklahoma City to Tulsa, so that when I came back, I could start over. A new town, a new life.''

''It couldn't have been that simple.''

''I did what I had to do, including giving my baby up for adoption. And later, when I'd heard that Johnny had crashed his fancy new car, I prayed that he had done what he felt he had to do, that he had died out of guilt. But that wasn't the case. He'd been drag racing with some buddies and lost control.''

''Adam isn't anything like Johnny,'' Sarah offered, watching Cindy twist her wedding ring again. ''He's good and decent, the kindest person I know. And this is killing him. With every day that passes, he dies a little more. His spirit is breaking, and I don't know what to do about it.''

The other woman's eyes filled with tears. ''Tell him I'm sorry. Tell him I did what I thought was best, what my family expected me to do.''

''He needs to hear that from you. He needs to know that you don't hate him.''

''Oh.'' Cindy rocked forward, touched a hand to her heart. ''I've thought about him over the years, at Christmas and on his birthday. He's always there. I haven't forgotten about him.'' Clutching her blouse, her voice shattered a little. ''I even nursed him. My aunt told me not to, but I did it anyway. I needed to hold him before they took him away.''

Sarah's chest constricted. ''He has no idea. He doesn't have that memory.''

''He's not supposed to. He has other parents now.''

''They're dead. They were killed in a plane crash when he was in college. You're all he has left.''

''Oh, no,'' Cindy whispered before her tears fell. ''What am I going to do?''

"Meet your son," Sarah told her. "If you don't, neither one of you will ever be the same."

With her emotions riding her sleeve, Sarah parked in her father's graveled driveway, unlocked the front door and stepped inside. She wanted to see Adam in person, but she'd offered to call rather than crowd him. Trusting him meant just that. She couldn't police him, even though a part of her wanted to. The whiskey incident had scared her more than she was willing to admit.

She set down her purse and picked up the phone. Adam answered on the second ring, which told her he had been waiting anxiously.

"Cindy agreed to meet you," she said.

"Oh, God. When? Where?"

"This Tuesday, at her house. Her other children won't be there, so it will just be you and her."

Fear jumped into his voice. "What about you?"

Sarah sat forward. "Do you want me to go with you?"

"Yeah. I mean, as long as you don't mind. You've already met her, and…"

He was nervous, she realized, anxiety-ridden about facing his mother. She pictured his troubled expression, pictured him pacing the motel room half the day. Was his hair banded into a ponytail? Or was it loose, a little messy? She wished she could touch him, run her fingers over those razor-edge cheekbones, that rugged jaw.

"Of course I don't mind," she said.

"Thank you." He paused, released an audible breath. "And, Sarah?"

"Yes?"

"You didn't tell Cindy, did you? You know, about what's been going on with me?"

"No. I didn't think that was my place." She leaned back, closed her eyes, suddenly nervous herself. How much time would pass before he lost the urge to drink? Before he felt whole again?

"Is she pretty?"

"What?" She opened her eyes, realized he was asking about Cindy. "Yes, she is. I think you're going to like her. She talked about when you were born. She held you, Adam. And nursed you."

"Really?" His voice turned soft, a little shy, and Sarah had to smile.

"Did she mention her other kids?" he asked.

"Only that they don't know about you. She didn't tell me their names."

After a moment of silence, he posed another question, shooting it like a bullet. "What about him? Did she say anything about him?"

"Yes," Sarah said, choosing her words carefully. Adam wasn't ready to hear details about his father. The wound was too fresh, the pain too raw. She suspected Adam had inherited bits and pieces from Johnny, physical traits that defined their gender. But none of that mattered. Cindy wouldn't look into her son's eyes and see the man who had hurt her. "His name was Johnny. He died in a car accident. He was drag racing with some buddies."

"I hope he suffered," Adam said, his tone cold and hard.

Sarah didn't respond. Hatred could destroy a person's soul, and Adam was still teetering on the edge of destruction. Despising a dead man, she thought, wasn't going to help him heal.

Thirteen

On Tuesday afternoon Adam opened the motel-room door and stepped back so Sarah could enter.

"I'm not quite ready," he said, stating the obvious. He sported a pair of tan trousers, but his chest was bare, his hair still loose. Adam rarely lingered over his appearance or criticized his wardrobe, but today he'd been doing both.

"That's okay. There's still time."

Sarah smiled, and he imagined holding her, breathing in her scent. He missed the feel of her, the warmth of her skin, the taste of her kiss. And today she reminded him of a gypsy with her shining black hair and glittering gold hoops. She rarely wore jewelry, but when she did, it enhanced her exotic appeal. He wanted to put a diamond on her finger, but he didn't have the right.

"How are you?" she asked.

"Better." Adam knew she was referring to his urge to drink. "It's not as strong as it was." But it made him realize how severe his addiction was, how he had downplayed the seriousness of it all these years.

"As long as you're okay."

"I'm hanging in there." He reached for a polo-style shirt and lifted it over his head. Turning, he headed for the mirror to band his hair into a ponytail. Combing the dark strands, he tried not to wince. His injured hand ached with the movement, and it shamed and frightened him that he was capable of such aggression. He wasn't the same man, and he knew Sarah deserved better.

When his hair was neatly fixed, he stared at his reflection and saw a stranger staring back at him. A ball of nervousness tightened his stomach. What if Cindy found him offensive. What if...

He spun toward Sarah, who waited at the desk, busying herself with a book he had left there.

"I don't think I can do this."

"What?" She whipped her head up. "Oh, my goodness, why?"

"I might have his face." He couldn't bear to resemble the man who had shattered a young woman's innocence. "My mother might look at me and see him."

"No, she won't." Sarah came to her feet and walked toward him, brushing his arm.

"How can you be so sure?"

"Because you look like Cindy. You look like a Cherokee."

"Thank you," he said, even though the knot in his stomach wouldn't loosen. No matter what Sarah said, he knew Johnny was inside him.

Wouldn't Cindy realize that, too? And if she hated his father, if her skin still crawled when she thought about him, then how could she accept the son who carried his blood? And how could Sarah? How could any woman?

"I'll get my shoes." He suspected Sarah knew more about his father than she'd told him, but he wasn't going to press her for information. He wasn't going to make her talk about the man who had tainted his genes.

Sitting on the edge of the bed, he laced a pair of leather ropers, then decided to change his shirt. "This one itches."

He peeled the garment from his body, knowing it wasn't the fabric. He didn't feel comfortable in his own skin anymore.

Adam chose a Western shirt, tucking it into his pants and threading a belt through the loops. Sarah watched him, and he felt self-conscious and nervous all over again.

They left the motel, and he offered to drive. The ride was long and quiet, but once they reached Tulsa, she read him the directions to Cindy's house. And when he parked in front of a tidy suburban home, he willed his heartbeat to steady itself.

The woman who answered the door was slim and pretty, with golden skin and hair the color of night. She wore her years with grace and style, reminding Adam of his other mother. And at that heart-clenching moment, he thought about how much he missed his parents, wishing they were standing here beside him. Unsure of what to do or say, he let Cindy take the lead.

"Hello, Sarah," she said, then turned to him. "Oh, my. You must be Adam."

He nodded, waiting for her to extend her hand. But she didn't. She just stood, staring at him, looking at every feature. Silence rose between them, like a ghost drifting on the wind.

He wanted to say something, to break the haunting, but he found himself staring at her, too. He did look like her, he realized. He saw the slant of his cheekbones on her face, and they had the same mouth, only hers was softer, painted with a peach-colored lipstick.

She wasn't as small as Sarah, but she was still a fine-boned lady, telling him that his father had been a big man. Adam stood taller and broader than most. Suddenly a sick feeling came over him, a need to apologize.

"I'm sorry about what happened to you," he said, his voice as raw as his throat.

Cindy blinked. "That was a lifetime ago." Reaching out to touch his cheek, she skimmed lightly. "Were your parents good to you, Adam? Did they treat you right?"

"Yes." He wanted to capture her hand and hold it, but she was already pulling back. "I loved them very much."

"That's what I wanted for you. A good life." Seeming a

little shaken, she smoothed her blouse. "Where are my manners? Come in, please, both of you."

Adam hadn't realized that he and Sarah were still standing at the door, the Oklahoma sun shining on their backs.

Cindy offered them a seat in a formal living room. Her home was bright and pleasant, with a vase of fresh-cut flowers on the fireplace mantle and a lavender-and-blue afghan folded over a melon-colored sofa. She appeared to favor pastels.

"I made coffee," she said. "And sandwiches. Would either of you like something to eat?"

"Yes, thank you." Adam spoke first. He wasn't hungry, and he normally steered clear of caffeine, but he'd heard it was rude to refuse food in an Indian home. He had no idea if Cindy followed the old ways, but he still worried about offending her.

"Can I help?" Sarah rose from her chair.

"No. No. I've got it. I'll just be a moment." The older woman headed toward the kitchen, and Sarah resumed her seat.

She and Adam glanced at each other, but didn't speak. She sent him a reassuring smile, and he wished things had turned out differently. He had caused sweet Sarah nothing but heartache.

Cindy returned with a tray, placing it on the coffee table. She poured the coffee and told them to help themselves to the food. The sandwiches, filled with a variety of meat and cheeses, were cut into small wedges, the serving platter garnished with greens and vegetable sticks.

Still nervous, Adam chose turkey and cheddar, then scattered some celery onto his plate. "This looks great."

"Thank you." She handed him a cup of coffee. "Did Sarah tell you that I have other children?"

"Yes, she did." He didn't see any photographs on the walls, but he assumed they were in a less formal room. A den, perhaps, where the family gathered in front of the TV. "I'm aware that they don't know about me."

"I'm going to tell them, but it might take some time. Rachel is only twelve."

Rachel. He imagined Cindy's daughter with big dark eyes and a pretty smile. "I understand."

"I'm not sure how they'll feel about all of this."

"You don't have to tell them." He poured milk in his coffee and tried to ease her mind. She looked as nervous as he was. "I don't want to make things difficult for you."

"They should know. I should have told them before now. Secrets can destroy a family. And I want them to meet you." She tilted her head, studying him. "You're their brother."

It was, he thought, the nicest thing she could have said. He smiled, and they both let out the breaths they'd been holding.

The conversation turned to small talk, with Sarah joining in. And when they rose to leave an hour later, Cindy hugged him.

Adam's mother felt soft and delicate in his arms, but at that tender moment, all he could think about was how much he hated the man who had hurt her.

Two days later, Adam drove to the garage where Sarah's father worked. He entered the office, telling himself he had to do this. He'd made some monumental decisions, and it was time to follow through.

A middle-aged man sat at a cluttered desk, the phone pressed to his ear. He nodded to Adam and signaled a gesture that said "I'll be with you in a minute."

He wore a dark blue uniform, and Adam assumed he was one of the mechanics who worked there. Checking his watch, he realized it was nearly noon. He hoped he hadn't missed William on his lunch hour.

"What do you need?" the other man asked, returning the phone to its cradle.

"Is William Cloud around?"

"I think so. Just a second."

Adam waited while the mechanic paged Sarah's father. This was the right thing to do, he reassured himself. The only thing to do.

William entered the office through a door that led to the automotive bay. They stared at each other for a moment.

Adam hadn't seen the other man since the day William had told him about the rape.

Sarah's father spoke first. "It's good to see you."

"Thanks. You, too. Do you have a minute?"

"Sure."

Since the other mechanic still occupied the office, they walked outside and stood near the front of the building. The garage was located in Arrow Hill, a wealthy community showcasing mansions and historical homes.

"I have something to ask you." Adam noticed that William watched him, waiting for him to state his business. He wasn't sure how the other man felt about him. They had barely gotten acquainted, which made this moment even more difficult. "I was wondering if I could go to one of those meetings with you tonight. AA or whatever it is you attend."

"Of course you can." William's expression softened. "So, have you stayed clean, Adam?"

"Yeah. But it scares me that it's become an issue in my life again. I never expected it to happen, not after all these years." He turned, met the older man's gaze. "And I've never been to a group meeting. I had private counseling when I was a kid."

"It's not so bad. In fact, it helps to know there's others out there. That they're struggling to get by, too."

"That's what I figured." But the idea still made him nervous, talking about himself to strangers, admitting that he had a problem. "I realize I can't hide from the truth. I need to get it out in the open."

"So have you told my daughter?"

"No, but I'm stopping by your house next." Which meant telling Sarah that he couldn't marry her. He hadn't officially broken their engagement, and he feared she was still clinging to false hope, to a fantasy about him that no longer existed. Adam was a changed man, born into a darkness he couldn't deny. Cindy was a kind and caring woman, but he was still Johnny's son, too.

"William?"

"Yes?"

"No matter what happens, I want you to know that I love Sarah. That I would never hurt her deliberately."

"She loves you, too. The way her mother loved me." The older man leaned against the building, but his gaze didn't falter. He kept his eyes trained on Adam. "And that kind of love is rare. One in a million."

I know, Adam thought, frowning at an oil stain on the ground. And that's exactly why he didn't deserve it.

Sarah and Adam strolled along her father's property. Hills rose in the distance, limestone mansions jutting from grassy cliffs. The rich, the working class. It was here that their worlds joined. Sarah was glad her father had chosen this area. It suited him.

Turning to look at Adam, she brushed a lock of hair from her face. Two days had passed since they'd met with Cindy, and now their time in Oklahoma was nearly over. She couldn't believe so much had happened within the span of two weeks.

"Our flight is scheduled on Tuesday," she said, praying that their relationship would resume once they got back to California. Adam was still withdrawn, at least around her.

He stopped, his boots layered with dust. "I'm not going. Not yet, anyway. Cindy asked if I could stay a little longer. We're trying to get to know each other before she tells her other children about me."

"That's good." Sarah told herself this wasn't the end. If anything, it was a new beginning. He would get to know his family and return to California a happier man. And then they could make plans for their future, decide where they were going to live, how many babies they were going to have. "So you rearranged your schedule at work?"

"Not exactly. I told them I wouldn't be coming back." He bent to pick a yellow flower, to hold the stem between his fingers. "I'm going to find a place here, focus on getting myself together. When I go back to California, it will be to pack and arrange to have the animals brought here. I have some time to find a job in Oklahoma. I've got money put away.''

''What about us, Adam?''

''I can't marry you, Sarah. You know as well as I do, we're not meant to be.''

She struggled to mask the overwhelming pain, the ache squeezing her heart. The man she loved was leaving her. For good. ''Why? Because you had the urge to drink?''

''That's part of it.'' He handed her the flower, then stepped back as if he'd crossed an invisible line. ''I'm going to a meeting with your dad tonight, but the idea of admitting that I'm an alcoholic makes me nervous. I've been hiding from it. Pretending the disease would never affect me again.''

''You'll do fine.'' She knew how important sobriety was to him. He'd gotten through the darkest moment of his life without a drink. He wouldn't falter now.

She brought the daisy to her breast. ''I trust you, Adam. And I'm willing to stand beside you, to help you.''

''I know. And that's what makes this so difficult.'' He frowned, turned to study the hills. ''You deserve better, Sarah. You deserve the kind of stability I can't give you. A home. Children.''

Stunned, she only stared. He no longer wanted children? A house in the country? How could a man change that much? How could he walk away from the woman who loved him?

Because, Sarah told herself a moment later, she didn't fit into his world anymore. She had been part of a dream, a fairy tale that had turned into a harsh reality. Adam was battling an emotional crisis, and she had no right to intrude on the time he needed to spend with his new family. They had become his focus, not a wife and children.

''I understand,'' she said, blinking back tears. She wouldn't cry, wouldn't beg him to include her in his life.

He stuffed his hands in his pockets, his voice raspy. ''So, what are you going to do?''

''Go back to California. My dad is getting along just fine. He doesn't need me fussing over him.'' She took a deep breath, fought the ache where her heart used to be.

"Have I thanked you?" he asked.

"A few times." She longed to hold him, to stroke his face, his hair, those broad, troubled shoulders. "I know you appreciate what I did." Convincing his mother to see him, she thought. That was the only bond they still shared.

He met her gaze, and she noticed his eyes still seemed vacant. He would win the battle, she reminded herself. He would be whole again someday. His new family would help him heal.

At the sound of shuffling feet behind them, they both turned.

"Hi, Sarah." Dillon Hawk, the fourteen-year-old boy from next door, came forward, holding his little sister's hand. She trotted along, her tiny face smudged with dirt.

"We picked some vegetables for your dad." Dillon handed her a brown paper bag, and his sister squinted into the sun, gazing up at the adults.

"Thank you. My father's at work, but I'll give it to him as soon as he gets home." After taking the bag, she introduced Adam to the kids.

He shook Dillon's hand, then knelt to greet the toddler.

"Hi," he said.

"Hi," she repeated, grinning at him.

"Her name is Rebecca," Dillon announced with pride. "But we call her Becky. She's almost two."

"Two," Becky confirmed.

She was adorable, Sarah thought, with her tanned skin and twin ponytails. A mixed-blood, just like Adam. And they seemed enthralled with each other—the big man and the tiny girl.

Sarah chatted with Dillon, telling herself she would survive this moment, the sight of Adam with a toddler who looked as if she could belong to them.

When the children finally left, Becky rode in her big brother's arms, waving and saying goodbye.

As they disappeared, Adam watched them go. "So they live in the farmhouse across the way?"

"Yes. Their father, Jesse, is a veterinarian. He has a practice behind their house and acreage that leads to the hills."

"It looks like a great old place. Full of country charm."

She nodded, realizing it was the kind of house Adam used to want. "Their mother is pregnant again. I guess they intend to have a passel of kids now that they've found each other again."

"What do you mean?"

"Jesse and his wife were separated before Dillon was born, but they're together now." Happy, she thought. Her father's neighbors were blissfully wed.

"Oh." Adam fell silent as they walked, heading back to the house.

When they reached the front porch, Sarah placed the bag of vegetables on a wooden step. A small breeze blew, stirring scents of an Oklahoma summer. She could smell hay, horses and flowers, like the one in her hand—a tiny yellow bloom from the man she would always love.

"Sarah?"

"Yes?"

"I'm glad you understand why we shouldn't be together, why you should have those babies with someone else."

Sarah's heart lurched, bumping her ribcage with a heavy knock.

Suddenly it all made sense. Every last, lonesome detail. He was letting her go because of Johnny. Adam still thought the blood that flowed through his veins was tainted. Meeting Cindy hadn't eased his greatest fear.

Sarah sat on the porch, and he stood by the rail, with those dark, vacant eyes.

"It's Johnny, isn't it? He's the reason you don't want to get married and have children?"

"He's my father, Sarah."

"He's a biological figure," she countered. "Not a father. There's a difference."

"But I inherited things from him. My height, the way I'm built. I'm not just Cindy's son. He's inside me, too."

"No, he isn't. You're nothing like him. And in truth, you

don't know anything about him. Maybe he was hurt or abused himself. Maybe he lashed out at Cindy because of his own insecurities, his own pain.''

Adam made a tight face. ''How can you excuse what he did so easily?''

''I'm not. By God, I'm not. But just because he was rich doesn't mean he came from a nurturing environment. He ran his car off a cliff, Adam. What does that say? Supposedly he was drag racing and lost control, but how can anyone really know what was going on in his mind at the time? Maybe he hated himself. Maybe deep down he wanted to die.''

His expression remained tight. ''And maybe he was just a selfish bastard.''

''Maybe,'' she agreed. ''But he doesn't matter to me. I'm not judging you by his actions. You're the same man you were before we found out about this. The same kind, honorable man. Your blood is pure, Adam. Pure and good.'' She stood, came toward him. ''And I want to have *your* children. I want them to be part of me, part of us.''

''Do you realize what you're saying?'' His voice sounded rough, flooded with emotion.

''Yes, I do. And I should have told you before now, but I was trying to make things right between you and your mother. Once she accepted you, I thought everything would be okay, that you would stop blaming yourself for what Johnny did.''

He sat beside her. ''How do I forget? How do I block those awful images from my mind?''

''I don't know. But you need to stop punishing yourself.'' She looked at the flower in her lap. It was so fragile, she thought. Like the human spirit. ''If a woman you cared about was raped, and she had a baby, would you hate that child? Would you think it was dirty? That it didn't deserve to be loved?''

''Of course not. I wouldn't blame an innocent life.''

Sarah moved closer, touched his shoulder. ''But don't you see? That's what you've been doing. Twenty-nine years ago, *you* were that baby. You were that innocent life.''

Stunned into silence, Adam stared at his bandaged hand.

Could it be that complicated, yet that simple? Was he destroying himself because he was trying to destroy Johnny? Kill a man who was already dead?

He lifted his gaze to Sarah and felt the sting of tears burn the back of his eyes. "I tried to right a wrong with hatred. I ignored the good my adoptive parents instilled in me."

"It's still there, Adam." She placed her hand over his heart. "Right there."

Blinking, he forced back the threat of tears. He hadn't cried throughout this whole ordeal, and damn it, he wasn't going to embarrass himself with watery eyes now.

He covered her hand with his, and while the sun shone bright in the sky and leaves fluttered on the trees, they felt his heartbeat, letting it flow through both of them.

"You had me fooled," he said, recalling the day they'd met. "You seemed like this confused little angel with a broken wing. But here you are, strong and beautiful and whole."

She smiled. "I don't know about the angel part, but I was confused. And if I'm strong and beautiful, it's because of you. You inspired me to give my dad a chance, to forgive him."

Adam thought about her admission, and then frowned. "I don't think I'll ever be able to forgive Johnny. I don't think I have that much good in me."

"Yes, you do."

How could she believe so strongly in him? Trust so deeply?

"Think about your parents, Adam. They didn't tell you about the adoption because they didn't want you to know about Johnny, to feed on the rage and shame you would feel."

He glanced up at the sky, then met her gaze, looked into her eyes and saw his future shining back at him. "Maybe I'll be able to pray for his redemption someday," he said, his voice breaking a little. "Maybe that will take the anger away."

She leaned into him, brushing his lips. "You're going to be fine. You're going to heal from all of this."

He tasted her kiss, the gentleness and the beauty in it. She was his soul, his heart, everything good inside him. Adam closed his eyes, opened them a moment later. "I love you, sweet Sarah."

"I love you, too. And I want to have a life with you."

His chest warmed. "Me, too."

She stood, held out her hand. "Then come inside. Be with me."

He looked up at her, immortalizing this moment in his mind. He knew what she was offering, what she was asking him to do. Sarah wanted to make a baby, to seal their union with everlasting life.

And he wanted that, too. More than he'd ever wanted anything. Accepting her hand, he let her lead him. It felt right to be needed, he thought. To be loved.

He smiled as she locked the bedroom door. Love gave you power, strength in yourself.

With a feminine touch, she began to undress him, baring his chest, unzipping his jeans.

Together they caressed and held, encouraging silk and sensation. And when they were naked, he took her mouth, long and slow. A kiss of friends, of lovers, of dreams and heart-filled promises. In each other's arms, they were home, safe and loved, where they belonged.

He licked her nipples, tasted and savored. Her hair fanned the pillow as his tongue slid over bare skin. Gold washed over the bed, the color of glitter, of sunshine and light.

He settled between her thighs, waiting to consummate their vow. "Say it, sweet Sarah. Say you'll marry me."

"I will." Lifting her hips, she took him inside, eager for the warmth, the deep, stirring penetration. "I'll marry you."

They linked their fingers, then moved in a dance as fertile and rhythmic as spring. He could feel life pulsing between them, the baby they were sure to create. Anxious and aroused, she gripped his shoulders, urging him to increase the tempo. And when he spilled into her, their worlds joined.

Afterward, Adam lowered himself into her arms and nuzzled her neck. She smelled like the wind and the grass and everything natural. Her hair felt like the flutter of a raven's wing against his face, her skin sleek and smooth.

"I want to have two ceremonies," he said, thinking about the future they had just sealed. "One in a church and one that represents the old Cherokee way."

Stroking his back, she slid gentle fingers up and down his spine. "There isn't just one Cherokee way. Different regions had different practices."

"Really? Like what?" He rolled onto his side, taking her with him.

"Sometimes it was up to a holy man whether a couple married. If he forbade their union, they would split up."

He frowned. "Forget that. I'm not going to let anyone take you away from me."

"There was also the proposal that was decided on by the maiden's mother. If the mother consented, the young man was allowed to share the maiden's bed."

He gave her a boyish grin. "I'm already sharing your bed."

She traced the shape of his smile. "And you declared your love at my mother's grave site. That meant a lot to me, Adam."

"I wanted her to know." For a moment, they were both silent, wrapped in a cocoon of emotion. He brushed a lock of hair from her cheek, and she moved close enough to increase the rhythm of his heart.

"We could exchange gifts," she said finally. "But it involves our parents. Your mother is supposed to give you something symbolic to offer me, and my mother is supposed to give me something to offer you. But since my mom is gone, my dad could take her place."

"That's perfect." It would be a new beginning for all of them, a way to bridge the gap that had separated them. Adam had found his mother, and Sarah had made peace with her father. And in nine months, he thought, sliding his hand over her tummy, there would be a child to bring their families even closer.

"Thank you." He leaned in to kiss her. "For believing in

me.'' For being there when he fell, when the addiction and the fear nearly destroyed him. ''I'd be lost without you.''

''Me, too.'' Her eyes turned misty, but he knew they were tears of joy. From now until forever, Sarah Cloud and Adam Paige would have each other.

He kept his hand on her tummy and smiled. As the Cherokee would say—she walked in his soul, and he walked in hers.

Epilogue

Sarah stood in the kitchen with Adam's spirited sister, preparing for an important party. She baked chicken while Rachel put the final touches on a relish tray. The counter was laden with food, from cheese and crackers to a frothy cake decorated with sugared roses.

Sarah took a deep breath. A garden window displayed a variety of potted herbs, enhancing the eclectic aroma.

Oklahoma was home again, and she couldn't imagine being anywhere else. Adam had opened a clinic in Tahlequah, an establishment that offered small-town warmth and holistic medicine. Sarah was also part of the business, adding natural skin-care remedies to the services. Everything she and Adam did, they did together.

Their charming old ranch house was filled with cats, and their yard flourished with plants. Two horses shared a small barn, whinnying every morning to greet the day. It was, she thought, the most beautiful place on earth.

"It smells good in here." Adam came up behind them, his boots sounding on the clay-tiled floor.

Sarah and Rachel shared a smile, then turned to acknowledge him. Sarah's heart bumped lovingly. He stood tall and
proud, a boyish grin tilting his lips. She knew how much he
enjoyed family gatherings, and today was special. So incredibly special.

"So how are my two favorite women?" he asked.

"We're fine," Rachel said, arranging carrot sticks just so.
"Busy doing women stuff."

"So I guess that means a guy can't mooch a snack or
anything?"

"Not on your life, buster. This is party food." With a satisfied smirk, the fourteen-year-old returned to her task, her
hair swishing across her shoulders.

Adam winked at Sarah, and her heart thumped again. Was
it possible to fall in love all over again? To see the sun and
the moon in your husband's eyes?

"I invited Jeremy to come by," he said. "And his parents,
too."

Sarah nodded. Jeremy was one of the teenage boys from
the youth center where Adam volunteered his time. He'd developed a warm relationship with the Cherokee boy, but they
shared a common bond. Both were recovering alcoholics,
only Jeremy's struggle was more recent. Of course, Adam
never forgot his challenge, and he never missed an opportunity to help someone in need.

Sarah's father remained strong and sober as well. He had
even begun to date, courting a woman who appreciated his
quick wit and easy manner.

Everyone was settled, she thought, happy and whole.
Adam's mother would be arriving soon to help with the party,
and his brothers were probably buying last-minute gifts. They
visited regularly, watching sporting events with Adam and
yelling at the TV the way men often did.

Sarah checked on the chicken, and Adam glanced at the
clock.

"Do you think the birthday girl is awake yet?" he asked.

"I don't know." She smiled and closed the oven. "Should

we go see?'' From the anxious expression on her husband's face, she knew he was itching to hold their daughter.

Hand in hand, they exited the kitchen and headed toward the nursery. Slipping quietly inside, they stood near the crib, silently awed. Kaylee Marie Paige napped with her bottom in the air and an empty bottle by her side. A cap of dark hair fell across her forehead, and her cheeks were rosy against golden skin.

Adam moved closer. ''I can't believe she's already a year old.''

''I know. But it's been an incredible year.''

''Yeah.'' He smiled at his wife. ''Being parents suits us.''

Just then, Kaylee roused, peeking at them through sleepy eyes. Adam reached out, and their little girl came to her feet, anxious to cuddle in Daddy's arms. He lifted her from the crib and held her close, brushing her cheek with a soft kiss.

Moving to stand beside her husband, Sarah said a silent prayer, thanking the Creator for each and every blessing He had bestowed upon them.

This, she thought, as Adam and Kaylee drew her into a family hug, is what life was all about.

* * * * *

Be sure to catch
Sheri WhiteFeather's next Desire,
coming in December 2001.

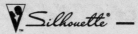

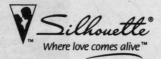

HARLEQUIN "SILHOUETTE MAKES YOU A STAR!" CONTEST 1308
OFFICIAL RULES
NO PURCHASE NECESSARY TO ENTER

1. To enter, follow directions published in the offer to which you are responding. Contest begins June 1, 2001, and ends on September 28, 2001. Entries must be postmarked by September 28, 2001, and received by October 5, 2001. Enter by hand-printing (or typing) on an 8 ½" x 11" piece of paper your name, address (including zip code), contest number/name and attaching a script containing <u>500 words</u> or less, <u>along with drawings, photographs or magazine cutouts, or combinations thereof</u> (i.e., collage) <u>on no larger than 9" x 12"</u> piece of paper, describing how the <u>Silhouette books make romance come alive for you.</u> Mail via first-class mail to: Harlequin "Silhouette Makes You a Star!" Contest 1308, (in the U.S.) P.O. Box 9069, Buffalo, NY 14269-9069, (in Canada) P.O. Box 637, Fort Erie, Ontario, Canada L2A 5X3. Limit one entry per person, household or organization.

2. Contests will be judged by a panel of members of the Harlequin editorial, marketing and public relations staff. Fifty percent of criteria will be judged against script and fifty percent will be judged against drawing, photographs and/or magazine cutouts. Judging criteria will be based on the following:

   - Sincerity—25%
   - Originality and Creativity—50%
   - Emotionally Compelling—25%

   In the event of a tie, duplicate prizes will be awarded. Decisions of the judges are final.

3. All entries become the property of Torstar Corp. and may be used for future promotional purposes. Entries will not be returned. No responsibility is assumed for lost, late, illegible, incomplete, inaccurate, nondelivered or misdirected mail.

4. Contest open only to residents of the U.S. <u>(except Puerto Rico)</u> and Canada who are 18 years of age or older, and is void wherever prohibited by law; all applicable laws and regulations apply. Any litigation within the Province of Quebec respecting the conduct or organization of a publicity contest may be submitted to the Régie des alcools, des courses et des jeux for a ruling. Any litigation respecting the awarding of a prize may be submitted to the Régie des alcools, des courses et des jeux only for the purpose of helping the parties reach a settlement. Employees and immediate family members of Torstar Corp. and D. L. Blair, Inc., their affiliates, subsidiaries and all other agencies, entities and persons connected with the use, marketing or conduct of this contest are not eligible to enter. Taxes on prizes are the sole responsibility of the winner. Acceptance of any prize offered constitutes permission to use winner's name, photograph or other likeness for the purposes of advertising, trade and promotion on behalf of Torstar Corp., its affiliates and subsidiaries without further compensation to the winner, unless prohibited by law.

5. Winner will be determined no later than November 30, 2001, and will be notified by mail. Winner will be required to sign and return an Affidavit of Eligibility/Release of Liability/Publicity Release form within 15 days after winner notification. Noncompliance within that time period may result in disqualification and an alternative winner may be selected. All travelers must execute a Release of Liability prior to ticketing and must possess required travel documents (e.g., passport, photo ID) where applicable. Trip must be booked by December 31, 2001, and completed within one year of notification. No substitution of prize permitted by winner. Torstar Corp. and D. L. Blair, Inc., their parents, affiliates and subsidiaries are not responsible for errors in printing of contest, entries and/or game pieces. In the event of printing or other errors that may result in unintended prize values or duplication of prizes, all affected game pieces or entries shall be null and void. **Purchase or acceptance of a product offer does not improve your chances of winning.**

6. Prizes: (1) Grand Prize—A 2-night/3-day trip for two (2) to New York City, including round-trip coach air transportation nearest winner's home and hotel accommodations (double occupancy) at The Plaza Hotel, a glamorous afternoon makeover at <u>a trendy New York spa,</u> $1,000 in U.S. spending money and an opportunity to <u>have a professional photo taken and appear in a Silhouette advertisement</u> (approximate retail value: $7,000). (10) Ten Runner-Up Prizes of gift packages (retail value $50 ea.). Prizes consist of only those items listed as part of the prize. Limit one prize per person. Prize is valued in U.S. currency.

7. For the name of the winner (available after December 31, 2001) send a self-addressed, stamped envelope to: Harlequin "Silhouette Makes You a Star!" Contest 1197 Winners, P.O. Box 4200 Blair, NE 68009-4200 or you may access the www.eHarlequin.com Web site through February 28, 2002.

Contest sponsored by Torstar Corp., P.O Box 9042, Buffalo, NY 14269-9042.

COMING NEXT MONTH

#1381 HARD TO FORGET—Annette Broadrick
Man of the Month
Although Joe Sanchez hadn't seen Elena Moldonado in over ten years,
he'd never forgotten his high school sweetheart. Now that Elena was back in
town, Joe wanted her back in *his* arms. The stormy passion between them
proved as wild as ever, but Joe would have to regain Elena's trust before he'd
have a chance at the love of a lifetime.

#1382 A LOVING MAN—Cait London
Rose Granger didn't want to have a thing to do with worldly and
sophisticated Stefan Donatien! She preferred her life just as it was, without
the risk of heartbreak. Besides, what could the handsome Stefan possibly
see in a simple small-town woman? But Stefan's tender seductions were
irresistible, and Rose found herself wishing he would stay…forever.

#1383 HAVING HIS CHILD—Amy J. Fetzer
Wife, Inc./The Baby Bank
With no husband in sight and her biological clock ticking, Angela Justice
figured the local sperm bank was the only way to make her dreams of having
a baby come true. That was before Angela's best friend, Dr. Lucas Ryder,
discovered her plans and decided to grant her wish—the old-fashioned way!

#1384 BABY OF FORTUNE—Shirley Rogers
Fortunes of Texas: The Lost Heirs
Upon discovering that he was an heir to the famed Fortune clan, Justin Bond
resolved to give his marriage a second chance. His estranged wife, Heather,
was more than willing to welcome Justin back into her life. But would Justin
welcome Heather back into his heart when he learned the secret his wife had
kept from him?

#1385 UNDERCOVER SULTAN—Alexandra Sellers
Sons of the Desert: The Sultans
When corporate spy Mariel de Vouvray was forced into an uneasy
partnership with Sheikh Haroun al Jawadi, her powerful attraction to him
didn't make things any easier! With every new adventure, Mariel fell further
under the spell of her seductive sheikh, and soon she longed to make their
partnership into something far more permanent.

#1386 BEAUTY IN HIS BEDROOM—Ashley Summers
Clint Whitfield came home after two years overseas and found feisty
Regina Flynn living in his mansion. His first instinct was to throw the
lovely strawberry blond intruder off his property—and out of his life. His
second instinct was to let her stay—and to persuade the delectable Gina *into*
his bedroom!

SDCNM0701